THE PATRIOT is a wonderfully written paean of praise to the power of love and the resilience of the human spirit in the face of overwhelming odds. Norman Weissman provides his physically and psychologically wounded men and women with a distinctive voice as they cope with finding love and life during World War II. His characters possess remarkable courage in dealing with devastating injuries and wartime experience that might overwhelm most people. His depiction of war, based on real events, some heroic, and others, like the Philippine Death March, horribly brutal, still others, farcically absurd, if they were not so tragic. His characters, heroes in every sense of the word, seek redemption for a nation that has lost its moral direction, perhaps even its soul. One hero, returning from home to the corruption and brutality of the New York waterfront where he grew up, takes up the improbable fight to reform it, while another of his wounded warriors challenges America's penchant for feeding its eighteen year old youths into the maw of misbegotten wars. *THE PATRIOT* engraves on the nation we have become, our debt to a wartime generation that struggled to find meaning amidst the wreckage of a world drawn inexorably to war.

Larry Dowler
Archivist, Yale University (1970-1982)
Librarian, Widener Library
Harvard University (1982-1998)

Norman Weissman's latest novel *THE PATRIOT* is a stirring tale that challenges the meaning of true American patriotism. Gone are slogans and the beating of drums. Instead Weissman's central characters are driven to self-sacrifice by their inner voices that demand morality and compassion in a world gone made with self-serving motivations. Profound and inspiring, *THE PATRIOT* is a book for all times.

> Myles Gansfried
> Playwright
> Author of:
> "Once upon a Park Bench"
> "The Computer Lesson"

A powerful and compelling commentary on the human condition and the resilience of the human spirit. A moving and exquisitely written story of the inward journey of three victims of war as they stagger through the darkness of their charred souls in search of hope, healing and love.

> Frank S. Patrick
> Author of : "Skin Graft"

At once both touching and searing, *THE PATRIOT* is an honest look into the travesties left in the wake of World War II and how they mysteriously unfold. Norman Weissman, master storyteller, captures intriguing historical detail and emotional complexities of characters that reveal how love, healing and hope can bloom in the most dire of circumstances. You will laugh and cry but not be able to put down *THE PATRIOT.*

> Maureen Goss
> Acupuncturist

THE PATRIOT's three compelling characters, wounded by the ravages of war, return to lead a vigorous peace movement, battle waterfront corruption and crime, and oppose the military's sexism and injustice. *THE PATRIOT* dramatizes the courage and imagination needed to restore the moral authority essential to democracy. A well-written novel clarifying today's troubling events.

Professor James Nee PhD
University of Massachusetts, Dartmouth.

Norman Weissman's intense feelings for American history makes *THE PATRIOT* a remarkable reading experience describing the futility of war. In a series of powerful and disturbing stories, Weissman creates unsparing portrayals of heroism and cruelty. *THE PATRIOT* is an exciting page-turner no reader will quickly forget. A remarkable novel by a forceful writer.

Herman J. Obermeyer
Author of :
"Soldiering for Freedom, A G.I's account."
"Rehnquist, a personal portrait of the Chief Justice of the United States".

"You are living quite a remarkable life – and have a wonderful ability to touch on significant events in your life portraying them in *THE PATRIOT* with an unexpected depth of feeling and knowledge."

Vickie Waymire, RN

The healing power of love, renewal and the resilience of the human spirit come alive in Norman Weissman's fifth novel – *THE PATRIOT*. He again fulfills his obligation to tell of the history he has witnessed challenging our concept of Patriotism by dramatizing the post war careers of an Army Nurse, a Waterfront Labor Organizer and a Peace Activist. THE PATRIOT is a "must" read. Bravo!

This is not the kind of story you would love to read. It is one you must read! THE PATRIOT captures the essence of the horrors of war as it was then, so it is now – asking the question – when will mankind wake up?

Also by Norman Weissman

The Prodigy
OH Palestine!
Snapshots USA
Acceptable Losses
My Exuberant Voyage

THE PATRIOT

A novel

by

Norman Weissman

Published in the United States by Hammonasset House
Books, Mystic, CT

Cataloging-in-Publication Data is available from

Library of Congress

History/Fiction

ISBN 978-0-9966169-1-1

FICO: 14000

www.HammonassetHouse.com

Printed in the United States of America

Book Distribution by Ingram

In Memory of my classmates

who did not live to 21

ONE

George Williams fought for his life at Walter Reed Hospital where pinging heart monitors and murmuring voices kept him awake at night. He did not ask for more than what one would expect from a critically wounded warrior.

"Blow the Bugles, beat the drums, Please someone, come and change my urine bag," he pleaded in a hoarse voice. "It's so full. So full. Won a Congressional Medal of Honor for Bravery you know. And tonight, another blanket please. I'm so cold. So cold. And when I look upon the world with sightless eyes and ask myself Why? Why? Why am I here? – there is no reply.

They say a great victory has been won! So tell me Nurse, what's the color of your eyes? Your hair? Are you tall or short? Do you enjoy your work? Are you married? Are you in love with some lucky guy?"

"Yes," replied the Nurse, a young Lieutenant, her blonde hair carefully tucked under her white cap. "I have met my man."

The patient nodded. "Joined the Navy to free the world and had my legs shattered. Returned with a brain that didn't work so good no more. Listened to crowds chanting USA! USA! USA! Singing *God Bless America!* Then jobless, homeless, with shadows on my soul tormented by loss, shame, and regret because I went to war a hero and returned feeling like a murderer. Tell me, where are you from? A small town? A farm? The Mid-West? The South? Do you look like Doris Day in the movies? She was my favorite Star."

A bell rang echoing down the hospital's corridors. An urgent voice on the PA system paged a Doctor. The Nurse leaned over the bed smiling as she placed a food tray on the patient's lap.

"Here's lunch – do you want me to feed you?"

"Hell no, I'm a big boy now."

The Nurse laughed, turning away to adjust the pillow. "Glad to hear that. Get back your strength and you go to Rehab."
The patient grinned. "Where they work miracles?"
"In six months you'll be walking."
The patient nodded. "And dancing? Will I ever dance again?"
"That's up to you," the Nurse replied as the PA system paged another Doctor. She turned to exit the room.
"What's the weather like today? Is it raining? Is the sun shining?"
The Nurse looked out the window. "It's a beautiful day."
The patient nodded. "I miss seeing the sun, clouds, blue skies. Can Rehab do something about that?"
The Nurse shook her head, gently touching his hand, fighting back tears. "I'm afraid not, but someday," she promised. "I'll dance with you."
"Like in my dreams dancing with Ginger Rogers?"
"Yes," the Nurse answered, smiling, hesitating a moment before saying – "Just like in your dreams."

His favorite recurring dream was soaring high above turbulent seas at night, flying formation on the Universe, with Orion his wingman. Arcturus guided him to the Big Dipper revolving around the North Star like the hands of a Grandfather clock. He called out his brother's name in vain hearing only the echo of his own heart's pain remembering his unlived years. He waited for a reply through the chill of wind and rain, hearing only the sobbing of silent tears.
"You must close your eyes and go to sleep," the Nurse insisted. "Tomorrow's another day. You need your strength." She fluffed up the pillows and cranked down the bed as the moon climbed above the distant horizon brightening the heavens with constellations unchanged since the beginning of time. George Williams had a vision of order, beauty, mystery and wondered, is this what dying is like?
"I'll see you in the morning," the Nurse said, interrupting his reverie. "Tomorrow I change your sheets."
George Williams recalled feeling like a child lost in the dark, flying another mission, a contagion of dread in the air he breathed listening to a voice spiraling down in a trail of white smoke diving

into the sea. With the transmitter ON he heard "Oh My God! My God! My God!" followed by silence that chills the heart like a burial at sea. A shipmate sewed into a white hammock eulogized by the lamentations of seagulls. Heads bowed, the crew lined the ship's rail holding back tears as the Skipper recited the 23rd Psalm. The Bugler blew Taps. The ship's bell tolled the eighteen years of a life that does not vanish into the ocean deep for Shipmates live forever, singing in the shower, like a radio that cannot be silenced. The off-duty watch pleaded for sleep, not a crackling voice or laughter shouting: "Shut the fuck up! No more singing – I wanted wings till I got those God damn things now I don't want them anymore."

The Nurse removed the food tray and arranged his bed for the night. Then he heard her write his vital signs on a clipboard before walking out of the room. He was familiar with her footsteps and voice and wondered – was she pretty?

In the hallway a Gurney rolled past his door. A shrill voice on the PA system paged another doctor. Outside his window life drove by with auto horns and sirens reminding him nothing changes, everything remains the same. He didn't need eyes to see that. He had seen the world. More than was good for him. He had seen the wounded and the dying, courage and cowardice, hope and despair. He marveled at the mystery of human resilience where the infinite possibilities of renewal are never exhausted. In despair he spoke to God to whom he said thank you for the gift of each day, but never for the nights. Long sleepless nights twisting and turning in bed talking to someone separate and apart from the one he knew himself to be. Another person. Another voice, harsh, assertive, judgmental, arguing, scolding, critical. It could drive him to the edge of madness. But no. He was not mad. Nor could he, without legs, ever be designated "walking wounded." He was only another G.I. with tragic stories to recall and tell. Sad Histories from the cradle but not yet to the grave. He was a solid citizen of the Great Republic who always paid his taxes when due and when told to go to war, he went.

"Do you want a pill to help you sleep?"

"No thank you, sleeping is the worst time of my day. Now I lay me down to sleep is like asking to go to Hell. I've got no benevolent God to keep or take my soul to some idyllic resting place. Awake or asleep, I'm in a purgatory where past and present meet at some painful point in time."

The Nurse insisted, "Your talking and shouting disturbs other patients. We must help you sleep."

The patient sat up and cried out: "Let me die," he pleaded. "Let me die."

The Nurse reached out and held his hand. "I can't do that, It's against regulations."

Her gentle touch stirred forgotten feelings of a caress, an embrace retrieving a primal emotion in his troubled soul. He raised his hand to her face tracing his fingers over her brow and cheeks and chin saying – "I can see you now. Yes, I can see you."

The Nurse laughed. "What do you see?"

The patient hesitated. Touched her lips, her throat, "You are beautiful, and young." He lay his head back against the pillow and smiled. "I guess I'll go on living. I like what I see."

Her soft lilting voice formed an image in his mind's eye and he remembered other faces young and old, homely and beautiful, sad and happy. With ten fingers he could penetrate the darkness and see where it is always night. And yes, he didn't need eyes to see the past which would be with him always and is never past. He counted her footsteps as she exited the room and tried to guess her height and weight. Not too tall. Probably thin, judging by her walk. Perhaps an Angel in disguise?

"Will I ever run again?" he wondered recalling his head back, swallowing mouthfuls of invigorating air, heart pounding against the walls of his chest. Legs reaching out in long strides with the cinder track unrolling under him effortlessly floating across the finish line, the crowds' roar fueling a final victorious burst of renewed speed. "Will I ever make love to a woman again?" he wondered, as he heard footsteps enter the room. "Will I ever hold a girl in my arms? How am I ever going to get to Berlin if I don't have a girl in my arms tonight?"

"You have had another restless night," the Nurse said, interrupting his singing. "Tossing and turning and throwing off your blanket. The Night Nurse tells me you were singing in your sleep."

The patient raised one hand, shaking his head, struggling to answer. "That's possible. Anything is possible. The singing in my head never stops."

The Nurse picked up the blanket from the floor spreading it on the bed. "What kind of songs – maybe one day you will sing one for me?"

"I have no voice. Can't carry a tune."

"I'm no music critic," she replied in a sweet lilting voice as he raised his head from the pillow and began singing a song he sang to another woman, in another time and place – "You're so much a part of me, a part of me, a part of me, the two of us are one. Yes. The two of us are one! Yes! The two of us are one! Yes! the two of us are one!"

The Nurse reached out and held his hand, her eyes tearing. "That's a lovely song," she said, remembering someone she gave her heart to but was now MIA, Missing in Action, or hopefully a Prisoner of War; a smiling face in a photograph she prayed to every night before going to bed exhausted, caring for men wounded in body and spirit gathering up the broken pieces of their lives. Disinfectant, Urinal and Bedpan odors invaded her life once sweetened by the Magnolia blossoms of her childhood. Her bedtime prayer – "Thank you for the World so sweet" – now evoked a smile, a laugh, a tear allowing no time to cry, turning her head, averting her eyes from Surgical Ward horrors. "Thank you for the Birds that sing" repeated again and again enabled her to concentrate on sponging up blood flowing from open wounds. So much blood, she thought saying – "thank you God for everything" – as if these words would banish what she witnessed. At night, dreaming, she returned to the world of a promising future with photographs of a wedding, childhood, adolescence and graduation evoking the lifetime she would never experience for her fiancé was gone, perhaps never to return.

"A sip of water please," the patient asked and she carefully poured from a pitcher filling a cup not quite to the brim, raising it to his mouth, reaching out to dry his lips with a face cloth. She also washed his face, combed his hair, brushed his teeth, a daily routine emptying bedpans and urinals, changing sheets, turning the patient over to prevent bedsores giving her life purpose, meaning, satisfaction. Grown men become small boys when injured. Pain obliterates all memory of adolescent years receiving her first surprising kiss. And when asked, she never hesitated to lean over and kiss the forehead or cheek of a wounded boy who was now all the boys of her childhood. A light quick kiss evoking a smile and a "thank you Miss" for she knew what it was to survive disaster, gasping for breath, kicking her legs struggling to stay afloat, swimming in an oil-soaked sea.

Thrown from her berth by a torpedo's fury, dazed, determined, she fought her way through passageways crowded with desperate passengers, reaching a deck where three thousand troops and eight hundred Nurses cried out, screamed and prayed as their ship rolled over and sank. Helen believed she was swimming amidst a thousand coconuts bobbing on an oil-stained sea. But no! they were the heads of soldiers, sailors and nurses struggling to survive the torpedoing of their ship holding on to each other in embraces that promised more than love.

Some survivors, insane with fear, cried for help fighting for life-jackets taken from the dead while others sang "Roll Out The Barrel – We'll have a barrel of Fun!" in a defiant chorus filling the dark night with hope. There was no laughter but many prayers, and when Helen was lifted into an overcrowded Life boat she said – "thank you God for sparing me."

An officer, struggling to keep the overloaded boat from swamping, threatened to shoot unwelcome boarders and when one climbed into the boat he pressed a pistol to the sailor's head and fired. Shocked by the sight of a body tracing a crimson trail on the oil-blackened sea the officer thrust the pistol into his mouth pulling the trigger to escape insanity.

The two hundred rescued would live their lives in gratitude and silence reluctant to remember and tell of the war's greatest Maritime disaster. She returned to her home town for thirty days "Survivor's Leave". A month living separate and apart from neighbors and family for she could not re-connect or resume the comforting friendships of childhood and adolescence. She had changed in ways beyond understanding, and walking once familiar streets, and crossing the Town Green she saw strangers. Clueless neighbors who welcomed her, nodding or shaking their heads at the miracle of her survival. She listened to complaints about gas and food rationing and doing their bit to help win the war with silent wonder for what can she say to complacent fools who never swam for their lives in the frigid Atlantic? She had no words to explain or bridge the distance between them, and when she realized no one was interested in what she could say she counted the days until she returned to active duty in Hospitals where few civilians visited. Warehouses of the wounded and the crippled, out of sight and out of the minds of patriotic citizens waving red, white, and blue flags at passing parades.

"What is your name?" the patient asked as the Nurse entered the room. "What is your name?"

The Nurse hesitated before replying "My name is Helen Christian."

"That's a lovely name" he said. "A lovely name." He turned in bed saying: "My name is George Williams like in George Washington, the Father of our country. I'm from a family of Patriots. My father fought in the first World War. His father in the Spanish American War, his father in the Civil War, his father in the Mexican War, the war of 1812 and his Father in the Revolution. That's a lot of wars, don't you think?"

Helen nodded. "Yes," she said. "Too many wars."

"Do you believe there will be more?"

"Yes, there will be more wars."

George Williams laughed, singing: "I'll take the Dames, let my buddies go down in flames, I'm no hero so I learned."

Helen applauded. "That's quite a performance. Where did you learn that song?"

"It's what we sing when we have had a bellyful of war. We're too young to die, don't you think?" Helen pressed two fingers on his wrist, looking down at her watch, counting heart beats, thinking she knew more than she would ever want to know about death and dying. Some go quietly to sleep and never wake, without a sigh or a death rattle in their throats as the last gasp of air flows from their lungs. Some fight for life with surprising energy struggling against the bedcovers, trying to sit up, pounding their clenched fists against walls only visible in minds experiencing their final moment of consciousness.

"If you behave yourself, and stop disturbing everybody with your singing, when I'm off duty tonight I will read to you."

George Williams laughed. "Bedtime stories? Jack and the beanstalk? Cinderella? Mary had a little Lamb?"
"You're impossible. The Ward's worst patient."
"That's me all right. My name is Trouble. A Hard Ass. A Fuck Up. First in war, first in peace and first in the hearts of my countrymen now living in darkness unable to see our beautiful world of Fairy Tales."

Awareness of life's pleasures came to George Williams playing with blocks on his mother's kitchen floor. Cabbage soup and baking bread odors, his father's voice, his brother's embrace, a hug and a kiss when he fell made him feel important as a child standing on two feet to confront the world with a smile. He had a happy childhood, a troubled adolescence and when he grew tall and slim he became a remarkably handsome young man. People turned heads to stare at him. Young girls flirted and a photographer so moved by his beauty displayed his graduation photograph in his store window for all the world to look at and enjoy. Listening to voices discussing cosmetic surgery, skin grafts and facial restorations he could not imagine his disfigurement.

He remembered hot searing flames burning his flesh, unable to see in a mirror he had no idea of what he looked like. He remembered how recognition of the horror of his appearance entered his room bearing the fragrance of a familiar perfume followed by his fiancée's uncontrolled sobbing. He waited in vain for another visit from the woman he loved who never visited again, revealing the truth about their future.

He remembered his mother, her tearing eyes and trembling hands, shaking her head as she read the document giving consent for him to enlist. Placing the form on the family Bible, she signed, sending another son to war, turning to him saying "this will keep you safe. Yes. This will keep you safe." He remembered November eleventh, Armistice Day, Church Bells tolling, his teacher reciting – "In Flander's Fields the Poppies grow between the crosses row on row" and he remembered high school classmates who did not survive with no "million dollar wounds" bringing them safely home but not sound in mind and body. He remembered his first date. Standing in her doorway, ringing the bell, a worried unsmiling father reluctantly welcoming a frightened adolescent about to carry off into the unknown his most precious possession. "Where are you going?" he asked.

"Radio City Music Hall, and we'll eat in a Chinese restaurant," he added.

"That will make her mother happy," the father explained. "She is more strict than I am about food." Riding the subway to Times Square on Saturday night was the night set aside for dating, holding hands, struggling to make conversation. "Next week is Regent's Exam week, are you worried?" she asked. He laughed, shaking his head. "They're not as difficult as everyone thinks."

The Chinese restaurant was crowded with other High School daters and she knew what to order. They ate quickly, praising the exotic food anticipating a stage show where a hundred "Rockets" in military uniforms, arms linked, marched across the stage, kicking their legs with breathtaking precision as the House Organ played *The Stars and Stripes Forever*. When the theater darkened to show the movie he held her hand watching Bob Hope sing "Thanks for the memory". Yes indeed. Thanks for the memory sitting so close together he felt her pulse beating with his. The subway was not crowded when they returned home to Brooklyn for it was only ten o'clock, an hour before curfew and lingering in the doorway she said "Thank you. I had a swell time" as he leaned over and kissed her before she fled into the house. A quick kiss. One he still remembered. He then thought about Connie, the most beautiful girl in his senior class, one he never asked for a date for her popularity guaranteed rejection. One afternoon, walking from school, to his surprise she invited him home and asked to introduce him to her mother dying of cancer who had been told they were engaged. A compassionate deception responding to her mother's most heartfelt wish. She showed him the ring on her finger confirming the lie she wanted her mother to believe. And when she invited him into her mother's darkened bedroom, the windows closed, shades drawn, he almost fainted inhaling the strong antiseptic odors of iodine and chloroform. The mother, a large woman, struggled to sit up in bed, raising her head to stare at him through tear-filled eyes.

"Congratulations!" she shouted. "How wonderful! Such a nice boy!" she cried out. "Now I can die happy!"

And indeed a week later he was invited to her funeral. A pageant of grief he did not have the courage to attend. He also thought about a classmate who disappeared from school. An unsolved mystery until his mother asked if he knew the girl confined to a dark room. Even the most subdued light triggered unbearable pain, crippling headaches, and she would now live in complete darkness for a year. For twelve months she would not see daylight or blue skies or green grass until hopefully, she would grow out of this malady and he thought how grateful she would be to see again. A great gift only the Blind truly appreciated.

Listening to talking books he was grateful hearing Tales of grief and strife, hope and despair, courage and fear so different from what played in the theater of his mind for his stories were never make-believe but real. They had no happy ending. Love did not conquer all. Heroes were not triumphant but destined to be bed-ridden, fed by tubes, peeing thru a catheter in their penis recalling moments in their lives beyond understanding.

He remembered Sylvia a withdrawn, solitary, dark-haired beauty ignoring the raucous revelry of skiers pounding the table with Beer Steins singing "The Bells of Hell go ding-a-ling for you but not for me!" Distanced from their inebriated joy she tolerated loud songs and crude jokes without smiling. A proper young lady not amused by vulgarity. Unattached. No one's date. Not interested in the romantic possibilities of a ski week-end. Defiantly alone mourning the loss of her fiancé, a Canadian Air Force Pilot. Grieving. She had attempted suicide. Been Hospitalized. And now skis all day, every day, no matter the weather, and after dinner goes to bed early, alone. He remembered writing a letter in the reading room dipping an old nib pen into an inkwell, dripping a large blot on the page. "Dammit to Hell" he shouted and from a large leather armchair nearby he heard laughter.

He turned as the sad young lady said – "Here, try this" handing him her fountain pen. "I hate those sloppy nib pens, they make such a God awful mess."

He finished the letter and returned the pen. "It's been a long hard day."

"Every day is a long day" she replied in a toneless voice. "For me there's no such thing as a short day."

"With a little luck some days are better."

"I wouldn't know about that," she replied and he remembered thinking about her unbearable sorrow. Do painful feelings freeze at a tragic moment in time and torment us forever? Does mourning ever cease? He recalled her dark hair framing an oval face, deep set eyes peering out from under heavy eyebrows conveying character, strength and sorrow. She seemed taller as she turned her head to look at him. After dinner the next evening he went to the reading room, borrowed her fountain pen and wrote another letter.

"You must have a lot of friends."

"Yes, I once had many friends. Some of them now dead."

They met the next day at the lift line sharing a double chair to the summit, bundled up against the cold in heavy ski parkas, peering out from tightly drawn hoods, wearing face masks and goggles recognizable only by their voices discussing the madness of skiing at ten below. After dinner that evening he went to the reading room with no intention of writing another letter. She sat in the armchair staring out the picture window at the skaters on a moonlit frozen lake. She offered him her pen.

"Not tonight, no more letters thank you."

"You will disappoint your friends."

"They'll forgive me, I've run out of something to say."

"I never missed a day," she said, lowering her voice. "I wrote every day without fail. Every single day."

"I'm sure you did."

She held up the pen. "This was given to me to write someone I loved," she explained, "a letter a day every day of the war." She paused. "Were you in the war? Were you hurt?"

"No."

"Why is that?"

"Some have luck. Some don't. It's a mystery."

"Yes." She said. Thinking for a moment. "It's a mystery. A great big mystery. And you can go crazy looking for an answer."

"Maybe you shouldn't look? Maybe it's better to accept a mystery for what it is."

"And what is that?"

"A question without an answer."

"I can't accept that."

"Why not? Why not accept there's a lot happens we'll never understand. Why should there be an answer to every question? Who knows why some live long lives and others die young? Nobody knows and nobody will ever know."

"That's cruel, not knowing."

"We can't know everything."

"Why do I know so much about pain? About sorrow? More than I ever wanted to know?"

"It's a mystery," he said again.

"I hate mysteries. I hate not knowing and I also don't like what I do know. I hate knowing my future. Miserable days. Everyone the same when you live alone. Bereft. Homeless. Without someone to love and who loves you four walls are a prison, never a home. Nothing ever seems right when a beautiful face, voice and mind you loved is gone and nothing remains but the excruciating agony of inconsolable loss. Unbearable sorrow. There is no tomorrow. Only yesterday when the good and the best die young and we live the lives given to us and wonder why?" She rose from the armchair and gazed out the window at a frozen lake speaking with her back to him. Her voice a cry of pain. Perhaps, he thought, a cry for help. "I've tried believing his death had meaning, some value. I wanted this terrible waste of a precious human being to add something to the lives of everyone who did not die for a lie told to the young by old men who send them off to war. It is not sweet to die for one's country." She turned from the window appearing surprised at his presence. Hesitating, she stared at him a moment, silent, thoughtful, suddenly reluctant to reveal herself. "We will never know what might have been, what our unlived years would bring. What our children would have been like. What kind of life would we have shared? What laughter? What sorrow? What thoughts? Would we grow apart or closer together? Would we love each other forever? What would we look like when our hair turned grey? Such questions are a cruel legacy of a life not lived. Of unfulfilled promise. Unanswered questions. A torment. Yes. A mystery."

The next day he skied alone. Made no effort to encounter Sylvia. Did not know how to respond to her grief. Did not understand his urge to withdraw. Break away. Not continue to witness her pain. He had learned more than he wanted to know about who she was and why she was here with no further interest in her sorrow. She entered the living room and sat next to him silently staring into the fire. "I heard you are leaving tomorrow."

"Yes, the new semester starts Monday." They were silent for several minutes, reluctant to resume last night's intimacy. He hesitated, searching for a reply before saying – "The saddest thought of all is what might have been."

"Yes. It might have been wonderful." She rose and stepped to the fireplace poking the burning logs with an iron. She turned and asked, "Do you know what day this is?" "No," he said, shaking his head, startled by the question. "Today is our anniversary. We were engaged a year ago today." The air in the room, heated by the blazing fire, became hard to breathe. The flaming logs flared. "I don't want to be alone tonight. – Not tonight." She stared at him awaiting a response.

He remembered searching for a kind reply as Helen entered his hospital room with a food tray. In a trembling voice he said: "I did not go to her that night. Or any other night."

"What are you talking about?" Helen asked. "Are you having another wild dream?" He shook his head. "Not a dream," George said. "Not a dream. Just something I can't forget no matter how hard I try. Something I failed to do."

"Remembering failures slows your recovery. You should only remember the happy moments of your life."

Helen Christian remembered her mother singing as she prepared her family's meals. She recalled the sound of pots and pans being scrubbed accompanied by a voice that seemed Oh so happy. The kitchen was a wondrous domain of bacon and eggs sizzling in a frying pan, water boiling and steaming and bubbling with freshly baked bread emerging from an oven delighting her young and happy heart. Happiness was in the air she breathed, an unforgettable childhood with affectionate parents who loved each other and their children. She recalled her first fearful school day, remembering the uncertainty of a strange new world of bells and harsh commanding voices, children shouting and crying, and when the teacher called on her she was speechless, unable to remember her name. She remembered her first true friend writing each other notes, sharing secrets binding them together forever in a pledge of eternal friendship. And she recalled her heartbreak when her friend moved to another town, another school and for many months she was sad and silent, withdrawn, refusing all offers of another friendship for she learned love can bring pain, pervasive sorrow that makes each day long and dreary. She remembered becoming aware of her body changing and the wonder of her mother's description of her future as a woman. She acquired a fascination with boys who would someday fulfill her destiny as a wife and mother. A mystery evoking fear and anger and desire and restless nights dreaming of what might happen if she ever fell in love. Life became a promise. She could hardly wait to grow up.

And then love happened. His name was Edward Cronin, everybody called him Ed, and he was tall, thin, with reddish hair and deep set eyes that looked at her with love and understanding she had never experienced before. They were High School Sweethearts who everyone expected would someday marry and raise a family and return to Reunions to reminisce about the good old days when they were young and careless. But that was not to be for all these possibilities were interrupted by war.

"Please don't go," Helen pleaded. "Wait until you are drafted."

"I'll learn to fly if I volunteer. Something I always dreamed of."

He held her in his arms seated on a bench overlooking Prospect Park's most romantic site for lovers.

"Flying's better than sleeping in the mud in the trenches."

"I'm afraid you'll never come back."

"Don't say that. It's bad luck."

"It's how I feel."

"Everyone says it will be a long war."

"I'll write you every day."

"And I'll write you in the morning when I wake up and at night before I go to sleep and dream about our future."

"That will be nice."

They turned to watch a horse-drawn carriage carry tourists through the park. A Police siren on the avenue wailed as it moved thru traffic. He gently slid his hand under her sweater and cupped her breast. "I like that," she sighed. "I like that." He kissed her as she reached out and held him closer. Trembling. "Do you think we should?" he asked. "I'm leaving tomorrow." She began to cry. Sobbing. "Yes," she said. "Yes. Yes. Yes."

The Bus Station was crowded with parents sending their sons off to war. Helen stood aside impatiently watching his mother embracing it seemed forever the boy she someday hoped to marry. His father waited for his turn to hold his son and say good bye, good luck, God keep you from harm as an American Legion Band played *God Bless America*. Then, breaking away from his parents he turned and opened his arms, holding Helen as she held back tears attempting a smile.

"I'll pray for you." She said. "Every night." He kissed her, a quick shy kiss and stepped into the Bus and was gone, perhaps forever she thought as her heart stopped beating chilled by pain. She remembered the first great love of her life celebrated last night, and prayed for the miracle of bearing his child. But that was not to be. She counted the days. And her prayer was not answered.

Helen Christian volunteered for Nurse's Training and in Anatomy class saw her first dead body learning how to prepare a corpse for transition from a Hospital bed to the Morgue after the final expulsion of excrement and urine. She learned to listen for the "Death Rattle", that last flow of air from the lungs that proclaimed the end of life. She learned to check all "vital signs", blood pressures, temperatures, feed and bathe patients, change bed sheets, prevent bed sores, empty urine bags, and assist bowel movements for the bedridden. After graduation Helen was commissioned a Lieutenant in the US Army Medical Corps ready willing and able to do whatever wartime duty demanded.

Ann, her favorite Instructor, after twenty years in Military Hospitals had seen every catastrophic combat injury. A tall commanding figure with prematurely white hair and an engaging smile, Ann mentored young Nurses who were unaware of the trauma they would soon witness. Idealistic Novices with youthful smiles and laughter who believed with time and loving care all will be well, so take your Meds and don't despair. Ann loved them all knowing the damage caused by years attending unrelieved horror. She remembered the moment when she was overwhelmed by the human waste of war and determined to prepare her students for an unforgiving future.

"Your greatest enemy is depression," she said, lecturing a class of newly commissioned Nurses. "And depression is insidious. A relentless enemy stalking you every working day. Silently attacking your composure without you being aware of the damage. Our casualties are not from bullets and bombs. There will be no Purple Hearts for nervous breakdowns and suicidal depression." The class shifted in their seats. A few nodded as if aware of the hazards they faced. The Instructor continued. "You must learn to distance yourself emotionally from what you see. Beware of pity. Don't confuse pity with love. And certainly it is hard not to mourn the death of so many beautiful young boys. Hardening your heart is not easy. Remembering their pain and smiles as they ask for help you are unable to give will be heartbreaking." Helen nodded and thought of her Fiancé who might now be wounded and unloved in some distant hospital bed. She began to cry thinking dying unloved unfair. The ultimate cruelty. But thank God he was alive and well and his letters reassured her they would marry when the war was over. She would survive the war undaunted and undamaged by the horrors of a military hospital.

"My Darling Helen", he wrote in familiar and reassuring handwriting. "Tell me what do I do when we meet? Do I salute or kiss you? Is there a regulation against kissing an officer? I must say being a G.I. has advantages. People are friendly. Buy you a meal or a drink or give you a ride when you're hitch-hiking. And I'm with a great bunch of guys eager to learn to fly. We're in an accelerated training program. We'll get our Wings after we log 150 hours about half of what it was in peace time. But not to worry. I'll soon learn to take-off, land, fly formation and let the Navigator do the sweating. They say it will be a long war but not everyone agrees. The Optimists say: "Home Alive in Forty-five!" The Pessimists say: "The Golden Gate in Forty-eight!" I don't know what to believe. Tell me, what do you think? I miss you. I miss you reading your poems to me. They were lovely poems. I wish I could remember them. Maybe you could send me some? I've written one for you. I hope you like it.

I found twenty-six stones
An alphabet, to build my bridge.
Ten thousand words I sent soaring through space
Crossing an ocean to your heart.
Writing not in ink
But in my soul's own blood
This my spirit you hold captive in your hand.
To this builder of bridges you reply –
I love you.
You look at me and smile
And all my words dissolve
Burning away at your touch.
Three words – a smile – a caress
Can say it all. Can bridge a lifetime. Can dispel despair.

Another sleepless night. George William's mind tormented him with foolish words from his childhood. "Georgie Porgie, Puddin and Pie, kissed the girls and made them cry, and when the girls came out to play, Georgie Porgie ran away!" This rhyme ran through George's mind over and over again and there was no way to stop it. "God dammit!" he pleaded, "Make them go away!"

Helen leaned over his bed and asked "What's bothering you? What do you want stopped?" George raised both hands to his head pressing them against his skull. "Those God damn words. Those fucking words are driving me crazy. You must stop them!"

"I don't know how," Helen replied. "Try to think of something else."

"There is nothing else," he shouted. "Just Georgie Porgie Puddin and Pie!"

"What is that ?" she asked. "What are you reciting?"

"A God damn Limerick only I was never Georgie Porgie and I never ran away when the girls came out to play."

"I can believe that," Helen said laughing. "I don't think you ever ran away from girls."

"You're no help."

"I do my best," she said. "But you must cooperate. There must be other things you can think about."

And yes, it was true. There were other events he would recall like working after school behind the soda fountain at Doc Barish's Pharmacy wearing a white apron and cap making and serving sodas, milk shakes, banana splits, ice cream cones and malted milks in a variety of flavors. Chocolate, Vanilla, Strawberry and Pistachio in ten and twenty cent portions. "One scoop or two" he would ask students with money, and for the embarrassed he served a "two cent plain". "The Poor Boys Champagne". A quick spritz of seltzer water flavored by syrup.

Doc Barish's was a popular after school rendezvous for High School Seniors reveling in their last carefree year after registering for the Draft precluding further study at the State University.

The store closed at six when George bicycled around town delivering prescriptions to the chronically sick and housebound who would call him son and gratefully tip and detain him for a brief conversation. Living alone, lonely, they opened their purses and slowly counted out and paid their bill while discussing the news of the day. George learned his customers were neither rich or poor and too proud to accept charity. On the far side of town inhabited by Irish and Italians and other immigrant families, he delivered prescriptions without charge and learned something more about Doc Barish's heart. A very human heart.

Doc Barish, a short, thin grey-haired Pharmacist wearing a white cloth coat and thick eyeglasses in steel frames could not afford Medical School. But that did not prevent him from practicing Medicine with only Pharmaceutical training. Frantic mothers brought him their children for stitches, splints, bandaging, baby teeth extractions and diagnosis of measles, whopping cough and fevers treated by aspirin or cough syrup. He also advised women with periodic problems alleviated by Lydia Pinkham's monthly pills. Enjoying his customer's gratitude, Doc Barish tolerated unpaid bills as a fact of life during the great depression.

One evening as they were closing the store, Doc Barish told George "If you apply to Medical School You would be exempt from the Draft."

"I don't have that kind of money," George replied.

"With your grades you could win a scholarship."

"I'd feel like a Draft Dodger."

"That's patriotic nonsense," Doc Barish insisted. "Our government needs Doctors as well as G.I's. My greatest regret is I didn't go to Medical School. I always felt I was born to be a doctor."

"Seems to me that's what you are now."

"Not really. There's so much I don't know. And George you are intelligent. Work hard. Do your job. I've often thought If ever I had a son he would be like you."

George smiled. Remained silent. Surprised by the compliment.

"Yes George. Believe me. I've worked hard all my life. Never had a family. Put aside a little money and have no one to give it to. I'd like to help you go to Medical School. I'd hate to see you go and get killed."

"I'm thinking of volunteering. Not waiting for the draft."

Doc Barish shook his head. "I know how you feel George. I was once very patriotic. Back in 1917 when we were fighting the war to end all wars. When good boys like you were dying to make the world safe for democracy a raging fever infected our beloved country. Liberty League Patriots sold war bonds and insulted able bodied men who were not in uniform. If you spoke German you were un-American. They even renamed Sauerkraut Liberty Cabbage"

"We're you in the Army?"

Doc Barish nodded. "I fought in Belleau Wood and the Marne. Saw more of death and dying than was good for me. Never was the same again. Felt I'd been deceived. Believed all these young men had died for nothing. That's why I say there's a better way to serve your country George. A better way."

George waited for Helen to enter his room, crank up his bed and place a food tray on his lap. With sightless eyes he turned his head watching her move around the room. "Would you believe I want to be a writer?"

Helen returned to his bedside and held his hand. "Yes. I would believe you."

He nodded and smiled. "Even though I'm blind," he asked.

Helen hesitated. Thought a moment. "You could dictate into a recorder and have your work transcribed."

"Who would do that?"

"Some good woman who believed in you."

George laughed. "You think that's possible?"

"Yes, George I do."

Helen walked to the door. Stopped. Turned to face George. "Tell me. Who will you write about?"

"You!" George shouted. "I'll write about you. How wonderful you are."

Helen smiled. Paused. Surprised. "George, are you flirting with me?"

"Yes," he replied. "You could be the love of my life. Just like in the movie where a wounded soldier and Nurse fall in love."

"That story didn't have a happy ending."

"Does it matter?" George asked. "They died for love!"

"Well don't count on me," Helen replied. "I have someone I love I'm waiting for. But tell me, what else would you write about?"

"Watchful waiting. Hours flying Combat Air Patrol, protecting the Task Force's outer perimeter. A dawn to dusk responsibility providing time to think - Kill or be killed! - a fact you live or die by when dueling with an enemy. Who will break off the attack first? - is the mortal question. The one who turns away first - goes on the defensive and the pilot who continues the fight - gets on his enemy's tail and has a chance to make a kill. Only with confidence can you kill him before he kills you. Without this offensive spirit you are lost. Just another pilot going along for the ride."

"It was a great victory," an ancient Poet said, describing a famous battle. But in 1943, in the Bismarck Sea, eight Japanese Troop Transports attacked by 90 Allied aircraft capsized and sank. Watching three thousand soldiers struggle for their lives George Williams did not enjoy killing men already doomed to die by drowning. The slaughter continued for hours. Squadrons of low flying American and Australian planes machine-gunned the enemy in a frenzy of revenge. Diving down to the sea for another strafing run, George shouted – "Let the bloody bastards die! They shoot

28

our parachutists, decapitate POW's or march them until they drop dead from hunger and thirst. God will certainly forgive me for what I am doing." And with his ammunition exhausted, his chattering guns silent, George Williams flew away from the blood-stained waters where war seemed like murder although fighting for the Right, flying into Hell for a noble cause was doing his duty by God and Country. War is Hell, he thought, although this is a good war saving civilization from another dark age of barbarism. Are we doomed to turn our cities into rubble, he wondered? Wars are corrupting leaving no one unstained. Pain and shame are the price of survival. As the poet said – it is not sweet to die for one's country – sacrificing millions of lives in wars threatening extinction. Cancers on a nation's soul metastasized by greed and the lust for power.

Helen did not enjoy the anguished moans, charred flesh odors and heart-breaking sobs heard in the Burn Ward. The wounded, bandaged in white gauze seemed like characters in a horror movie evoking repellant feelings Helen could not emotionally distant herself from as she dispensed narcotics that failed to subdue pain. In other Wards there were smiles, jokes and laughter moderating the agony of catastrophic battle wounds, amputations, and surgeries. The Burn Ward seemed a dark and forbidding place where a comatose soldier, his face concealed by thick layers of gauze, moaned and groaned. Without "Dog Tags" or other clues to his identity he was listed as an "Unknown Soldier" without name, rank or serial number. Who was he? What was his nationality? Who were his next-of-kin? What was his age? The patient who could not speak became an iconic presence, an inert body challenging Helen's imagination, stirring her innocent young heart. Whenever she came to his bedside she felt something familiar, recognizable and attractive in this soldier who could be any one of hundreds of young men arriving at the hospital every day. These feelings intensified, became undeniable and compelling when she thought of her fiancé reported MIA, Missing in Action. She feared it might be Edward concealed under the bandages as she unwrapped the gauze to apply burn ointments to charred flesh. She felt relieved this grotesque face was not the man she loved. The man she hoped to marry. Holy Mother of God! she thought. What are we doing to these beautiful boys who are so injured, brave and patriotic? What will happen to them when the killing stops? She began trembling, sobbing, and impulsively reached out to grasp the Unknown Soldier's hand seeking comfort and reassurance from touching another human being. Connecting to another life.

Her supervisor, Nurse Ann, walking past the bed on her rounds stopped and turned to Helen saying quietly "What you are doing can ruin you. It's a fool's game becoming emotionally involved. There will be hundreds of these dying boys, and you must learn to accept the fact we will lose more than a dozen every day. Do not make one patient more important than another. You have no time for love or mourning."

"What a horrible thought," Helen said withdrawing her hand. Shaking her head. Disagreeing.

"It's the Truth," Ann replied. "Nothing but the truth."

"I can't turn off my feelings," Helen insisted fighting back tears.

"You have no choice. You're a Nurse, not a schoolgirl." Ann replied reaching out to embrace Helen with an affectionate maternal embrace.

"I'm a human being who can't forget what I see, Helen sobbed. Can't stop being who I am."

Nurse Ann stepped back releasing Helen. "I once felt that way," she said, remembering – "almost killed me. Couldn't eat or sleep. Had nightmares dreaming the dead came alive when I prayed for them. Held their hands. Spoke to them as if what I said to God would keep their hearts beating. Felt possessed by the power of life or death before I collapsed into madness and was six months before I could return to duty." Ann hesitated, searched for words. Pleaded. "Can't afford to lose you Helen. There's too much to do and too few Nurses to do what must be done. Be professional. Cold and distant and do what you have been trained to do. Believe me, that's not asking too much."

Morning in the Burn Ward. Patient's awakening. Nurses emptying bed pans. Taking temperatures. Retrieving bed covers. Adjusting pillows. Cranking up beds. Moans groans and suffering.

George winced as the bandages were removed. What do I look like?" he asked. "Am I ugly?"

I've seen a lot worse," Helen responded spreading ointment on burnt flesh covering his cheeks, throat and forehead.

"What are you doing?" he asked, feeling pain. "What's that God-awful smell?"

"Burn ointment to protect your wound while you grow new skin."

"Grow new skin?" George said. "Is that possible?"

"Removing charred flesh accelerates healing," Helen explained.

"Always?" George asked. "Does burnt skin always heal?"

"When there's no infection."

George nodded. Reassured. "When will you uncover my eyes?"

"When the Doctor says you're ready."

"When will that be?"

Helen hesitated, reluctant to reply. She reached out and held his hand. Her voice soft and comforting. "Your eyes are gone, George. We couldn't save your eyes."

George groaned. Shaking his head. Fighting back tears. Then, hesitating he asked: "What about my face? Do I look like a Monster? Will I frighten children and dogs?"

"With new skin and grafts, you will look good."

"How good?"

"Good enough for all normal purposes."

"That's nice to hear" George said. Encouraged. Fighting despair.

"You'd be surprised how good patients look when they leave the Burn ward."

The PA system paged a Doctor. Announced Orders of The Day. Reported Time and Weather. Played soft music. A Gurney rolled into the Ward with another patient.

"George raised his head from the pillow. Speaking quietly. Pleading. "There's something you must do for me."

"What's that?"

"No visitors. I don't want anyone to see me until I'm healed."

"We can't prevent your family and friends from visiting."

"I have no family and all my friends are dead."

"Then what's the problem?"

"I don't want my fiancée to see me. The shock could kill her"

"How can you say that?" Helen demanded. "Maybe she's braver than you think?"

"I don't want her to marry me out of pity."

"What if she loves you?"

"She'll get over it. She's young. She'll find a better man."

"And what about you George? Do you love her?"

George nodded. "I don't want to ruin her life."

Helen replaced the bandages. Remained silent for a moment. Then, before exiting the room, she turned and said: "You must allow her to visit, George. Maybe what she feels is true love and not pity? You'll never know if you keep her away."

George hesitated a moment before replying, "She's been here" he said, recalling the familiar odor of perfume invading his room, her sobbing, and silence, and footsteps walking away from his beside. "She may try to see me again."

George knew he was fighting for his life counting footsteps entering his room noticing how some visitors stopped, turned and moved to the far side of the bed distancing themselves from him. Struggling to stay alert despite medications dulling his brain, he identified Doctors and Nurses by their walk. Some came for a fast look, made a few sympathetic comments and then retreated. Yes. It would be a long battle. Maybe years. So take your meds and don't despair. Tomorrow is another day. And who said a blind man can't see?

Big Jim, his Physical Therapist, was over six feet tall, weighing 255, with a deep bass voice and a reassuring smile. Whenever he entered the room, George felt comforted by someone who sustained his hopes of recovery. He welcomed Big Jim's strong arms when lifted out of bed and into a wheel chair. Shouting "Away we go!" he pushed George down the hallway to Rehab where he learned to walk on prosthetic legs. George Williams was a compliant patient during the six months needed for his incisions to heal and the swelling of his residual limbs to subside. Skilled technicians precisely fitted his residual limbs into prosthetic leg sockets taking care to prevent skin irritation, discomfort, and tissue damage. A bad fit caused pain, sores, and blisters. With the fabric liners retaining body heat, perspiration needed several hours every day without the prosthetics, to dry. Preventing Limb movement within the socket required several fittings to accommodate shrinking residual limbs.

"But first we must strengthen your arms and shoulders," Big Jim explained. "Your muscles atrophy after months in bed and when you don't have legs, strong arms are a man's best friend getting you out of bed, off the potty, and in and out of a chair. You'll soon be walking if you work hard and never give up! Believe me some prosthetics like Doug Bader fly again and shoot down Germans or fight the war from behind a desk. So never give up and someday you can run a marathon if that's what you want."

"I'd like that."

"We got prosthetic runners, basketball players, skiers, and mountain climbers doing whatever they want to do."

"Can a blind man run?"

"Everything's possible if you set your mind to it."

"I ran in High School. Won the hundred meter dash," George said. "Got a Gold medal."

"Basketball was my sport," Big Jim explained. "Didn't matter I was black as long as I was tall. Wearing prosthetics all men are equal. Black. White. Brown. Yellow. It's what's in your head that matters. Some patient's think their lives are finished believing they're not good for anything. They've forgotten where there's hope there's life if you never give up. Some weak souls just roll over, turn their face to the wall and die. It's like something inside them was already dead. And some men go on living making the most of God's precious gift! It's the fight for life and I've seen men choking on their own blood as they struggle to take their last breath. Not a pretty sight. But what is given to us will sooner or later be taken away and it's not for us to say when."

George wondered is it possible to fall in love with footsteps, a voice, a gentle touch, a female presence. For that was the only evidence of Helen's existence. Helen asked herself can a woman truly be in love with two men? Her feelings for her fiancé were deep, emerging from the dark mystery where true devotion gestates. Re-reading his letters and poems she heard his voice, saw his smile, felt the embraces that stirred her memory of bodies pressed together in rising passion. "MIA. Missing in Action," the telegram said. The Secretary of War regrets to inform you your life's greatest joy may be dead. Now you live with an emptiness that knows no replenishment. Long days, sleepless nights, working without satisfaction or pride, Helen distanced herself from the wounded. Children for whom she no longer felt maternal. She hated the war. Could not forgive the waste of young lives. She never learned to defeat loneliness. There was no release from being alone. She often paused in her work to touch the wrist bracelet bearing Ed's name praying for news of his fate. Some certainty he was alive or dead. Not knowing was perpetual mourning without closure. Pain stalked her waking moments with a rising tide of sorrow tormenting her. Seeing patients embraced and kissed by visitors, she envied their devotion and prayed that Ed would soon appear and greet her with open arms and a smile. I'd walk a million miles for one of your smiles were lyrics she remembered searching back into her past to find the strength she needed to continue living. But how many footsteps are there in a million miles? A journey of a million miles begins with a single step. But what is that first step?

Pharmacist Mate Big Jim, was one of the first Blacks so rated in a Navy restricting men of color to a Seaman's rank. "Medics" were battlefield heroes and on ship's without doctors performed appendectomies and treated wounds saving lives with immediate care. Assigned to work in Rehab, training patients without arms or legs, Big Jim's strength enabled him to carry them from bed to exercise table and treadmill where they learned to walk with prosthetics. But first he broke their silence urging patients to talk.

"Where are you from? How did this happen? How do you feel?" he asked. Humorous banter overcoming with laughter the tragedy of no arms or legs.

"Yes, shit happens but we can do something about it!" were encouraging words fighting withdrawal and despair. When fitting prosthetics to residual limbs Big Jim explained with a smile – "You can get any color you want as long as it's black." And after receiving a laugh or a nod in reply he asked: "too loose? too tight?

just right?" like an enthusiastic salesman selling a beneficial product.

Restoring muscular strength on the exercise table Big Jim supervised sit-ups, leg lifts, and push-ups. The choreography of recovery repeated daily for months, rebuilding bodies for a return to an unknown future.

With his first tottering steps, standing upright between Parallel bars, George Williams learned how he held his head maintained balance. Looking down with sightless eyes as if to see his feet, he'd fall. Staring straight ahead he walked confidently, discovering the gift of mobility even though blind. Big Jim shouted encouragement. "That's right," he said. "That's right! The balance of the body is how you hold your head. Your gonna go where you look. Look down at the ground and you'll fall on your face. It ain't easy. Stop worrying about where your feet are. It's heel and toe and away you go! And before you know what's happening, you're walking."

Stepping out from between supporting parallel bars, prevented from falling by a movable harness attached to an overhead trolley, George walked across the room on his prosthetics. Big Jim applauded. "Zippidi Do Dah! Zippidi day!" he shouted. "Zippidi Do Dah! Zippidi day! Just forget about how you place your feet. They'll do right if you walk straight and tall like you own the world and nothing's gonna defeat ya. I've seen this happen more than a hundred times when you open the door to your heart and spirit everything's possible. I tell you it's a gift you must hold on to and never let go. A great good gift of God trying to rebuild this fucked up world one body at a time. One body at a time. That's why I do what I do, knocking on the door to your heart so you'll open it and never except defeat. Never! – 'cause the heart always knows the way home."

Weekly "Mail Call" was always a disappointment for Helen hearing the Battalion Postal Clerk call names receiving food packages and letters. She envied Nurses shouting like school girls as they rushed forward to grasp the gifts of family and friends for letters were more important than food and Helen's pain at not hearing her name was devastating. Next week, she told herself, next week a letter from Ed would come contradicting the report he was MIA. Missing in Action. A possibility she refused to accept until a telegram chilled her heart as she shouted No! No! No! reading – "The Secretary of War regrets to inform you Private Edward Sullivan USA is now KIA, Killed in Action. Further information will be sent as received." Helen blacked out. Fled reality for three unconscious days. Revived and sedated, she returned to active duty with a wound that would never heal.

Helen Christian never trained as an anesthetist and was surprised when assigned to replace a surgical nurse administering ether during an amputation. When the surgeon made an incision in the skin and underlying tissues she fought nausea watching him tie-off bleeding arteries. As he folded back a flap of skin over a shattered knee, Helen determined not to faint. All she remembered after falling to the floor was the sound of a surgical saw cutting deep into bone and the sharp crack of a sawed-off limb separating.

Helen welcomed reassignment to the 31st First Infantry Battalion Aid detachment, a frontline medical unit of two combat surgeons, eight Nurses, ten Medical Orderlies and fifteen Litter Bearers. Located two thousand yards behind fighting troops Helen endured the deadly bombing and strafing of a combat soldier while administering Plasma to prevent shock and injecting morphine to ease pain. The wounded she "stabilized" were then sent to Division Collecting Stations where skilled surgery and more intensive care saved lives. To escape falling mortar shells and shrapnel, Helen sheltered in a Foxhole sleeping whenever there was a break in the arrival of Litter Bearers bringing casualties to her First Aid station. Overwhelmed by the increasing number of wounded, assessing each soldier's possible survival, granting or withholding treatment, was a difficult decision for soldier's denied immediate care never survived. "Triage", choosing who would live and who would die was never taught at Nursing School. Head wounds with half a brain shot away, armless legless basket cases with their intestines cascading out of their bellies were considered hopeless, beyond repair. Saving lives was a joyous responsibility. The source of Helen's pride as an Army combat Nurse for she had been taught to save one life is to save the world.

The Nurses in Helen's medical unit were bonded by the horrors of war and the anguish of watching young boys die. Helen became a battle-hardened veteran accompanying combat troops wading ashore at Morocco, and then fighting two hundred miles across North Africa to Tunisia, enduring heavy casualties until finally checked at Kasserine Pass where well-trained, disciplined German Panzers routed inexperienced and poorly equipped G.I.'s who panicked, turned and fled the battlefield. Helen retreated with them to a rear area Hospital where she was ordered to remain with the wounded and be captured. The attacking Germans, running out of fuel and ammunition, halted. The Americans regrouped and succeeded in establishing a new defensive frontline where Helen resumed saving lives.

During lulls in the fighting the Nurses shared their food parcels, read letters from home, washed their hair and sang sentimental songs evoking laughter and tears in a momentary escape from war. Scotty, a tall attractive Army Nurse maintained morale by her cheerful presence and a commanding voice that silenced despair. She led them singing *Don't sit under the apple tree with anyone else but me.* Her instinctive leadership set an example everyone followed. Death was a fact to be accepted. War is Hell, a tragedy they confront every day. When German artillery and planes ignored the Red Crosses on hospital tents, bombing and strafing in violation of International Law, the Nurses minimized the danger, confident they would survive. Helen soon discovered another kind of love, a growing attraction for Scotty, a tall, thin soft-spoken beauty who seemed withdrawn into herself, unflappable during bombings. Sharing Foxholes and a bedroll with Scotty, seeking the warmth of another body during cold Tunisian nights, their proximity evoked feelings different from those she felt for her fiancé. She felt safe, loved, comforted. Prayed this happiness would never end. Caring for patients during the day, Scotty and Helen never acknowledged their feelings for each other quietly looking forward to the night.

In a world producing more weapons, more bombs, more destruction, where nations continue bombing each other, there is no sanctuary for lovers. An artillery shell exploding inside the Surgery Tent dispersed shrapnel ending Scotty's life as she worked to save a German prisoner whose racially pure blood was now mixed with hers. Grieving. Shocked. Helen was ordered to prepare Scotty for collection by the Graves registration company for burial in the American Military Cemetery in Tunisia where a Star of David and a metal plaque recorded her name, rank, serial number, date of birth and death. Fighting back tears. Helen tenderly washed Scotty's blood stained body, carefully dressed her in a clean uniform, combed her hair, and mournfully kissed the cold lips that once brought such joy to her now broken heart.

Great sorrow is often more destructive than bombs. Without Scotty, Helen felt half alive.

Her stoic composure replaced by a tantrum impatience with frustration. A constant dread and rootless fatigue, bogus pains and nervous tics made her appear to be a shell-shocked survivor. She began to stutter and found work unbearable. Each death a personal defeat wondering if she had done everything possible to save that life, that boy, that father of a family back home who were unaware of his fate. When pronounced dead, she prepared corpses for burial and returned to work on the living with despair in her no longer young and tender heart. And when a soldier she thought dead was placed in a body bag and lowered into a grave – cried out – cursing Helen's mistake – she collapsed, overwhelmed by the horror of her error. Evacuated to a rear area hospital, Helen was placed on a suicide watch. And the life she now fought to save was her own.

After a long day working as a Rehab specialist, Big Jim often recalled life as a Share Cropper Cultivating land he did not own for sharecropping was the only choice for poor whites and emancipated slaves after "Forty Acres and a Mule" became an unfulfilled promise.

Sleeping on a Corn shuck mattress in a one room shack, shitting in an Outhouse Privy, drinking from a contaminated well, Big Jim's childhood heritage was an aching back and hands blistered picking cotton. Comforted by his mother saying "blessed are the poor and humble for they shall inherit the earth" Big Jim accepted hardships he could not change. At sundown he sang – "Massa won't you ring that bell" welcoming the end of a day made bearable by singing Gospel songs led by a charismatic Preacher who promised "Pie in the Sky when you die." In the one room school house he attended when not working, an inspiring teacher encouraged students to go North. "Follow the drinking

Gourd," she said, "The Big Dipper will show you the way to a better life."

Big Jim rode the rails North to the Promised Land of factories, skyscrapers, slums, and low wage jobs. He dug ditches, paved streets, washed windows, and hauled ashes from furnaces providing heat and light in cities where he never again sang as he worked. And when exploited white Industrial workers went on strike, Big Jim escorted by National Guardsmen crossed Picket lines becoming a Strike-breaker enduring the hatred and damnation of men struggling for the better life he dreamed of. Big Jim also encountered men who kept that dream alive marching protesting and singing, *We Shall Overcome,* choking on tear gas, attacked by police dogs, clubbed to the ground carrying signs proclaiming "I AM A MAN ! I AM A MAN !"

Yes, Big Jim agreed – I am a Man with thoughts, feelings and dreams like other men.

Born again, he no longer accepted the role society assigned to him. Overworked, underpaid, exploited, Big Jim acquired the dignity of knowing he possessed equal right to life, liberty and happiness. Even he was entitled to some happiness, he thought. Proclaiming – "I am a Man" he became a Man.

Aaron Fechter, a small man, had big ideas. Proud and generous proprietor of Fechter's Bookstore, he thought books the most complex and greatest of all wonders created by man on his path to happiness and a greater future. He could not consider any other way of earning a living. From nine in the morning to ten at night, he greeted and advised customers with a surprising instinct for what they were looking for. As one of "The People of the Book", raised on the Torah and the Talmud, Aaron Fechter believed books transmit human experience from generation to generation becoming a nation's living memory preserving and protecting its soul. For Aaron Fechter books were never inanimate objects but living, speaking treasures as rich and diverse as humanity, as complicated and captivating as life itself. Affectionately called "Old Aaron" by his customers he never confessed his age, although a shuffling walk and white hair betrayed eighty years.

Pedestrians looking into his window to glance at his book display disappointed him when they walked on without entering the store. Some became familiar, students, housewives, workers, businessmen who stopped and then vanished into the passing crowd. Like hungry children at a candy store, some peered into the window several times a week. A tall negro wearing overalls and a sweat- stained bandana around his neck often stopped and stared at books with wonder and surprise. Another passionate book lover Aaron Fechter thought, hoping to see him again. One evening he opened the door and invited him into the store.

"Do you know about our free Lending library?" Aaron asked, smiling. "There is no charge as long as you return books undamaged."

"Free books?" Big Jim asked, surprised at the friendly invitation.

"Yes," Aaron explained respectfully. "It's how we encourage new readers to someday become customers."

"I don't know nothing about books," Big Jim replied, "wouldn't know what to ask for."

"I can help," Aaron said. "I'm good at finding books for people."

And so Big Jim's education beyond reading and writing and arithmetic began as a reader in a Lending Library created by Aaron Fechter's generous heart in a society where blacks were denied access to Public Libraries. For Big Jim Mark Twain, Jack London, Langston Hughes, Richard Wright, and Ralph Ellison evoked disturbing thoughts and feelings about the destructive power of hatred. Big Jim began to understand his anger. Kipling's "If you walk with crowds and keep your virtue" promised a life Big Jim now thought possible in a world where everything now seemed possible. He felt at home in a white man's world knowing he had a place in that world. Education enabled him to understand Langston Hughes writing – "I count it little being barred from those who undervalue me, I have my own soul's ecstasy." Reading became Big Jim's ecstasy.

Enlisting in the Navy, tested and evaluated for assignment to some duty more challenging than a Cook or Steward, Big Jim trained as a rehabilitation Medic. The Rehab Ward became his Church. Patients were Parishioners in a congregation restoring broken bodies and shattered spirits believing no hope was beyond attainment. Like a benign God, Big Jim, now a "Miracle Worker", revitalized courage and dispelled despair loving his work. The gratitude he received rehabbing patients became pure joy.

One day George Williams asked, "Don't you ever tire of the monotony of Rehab work? I should think it would drive you mad repeating these exercises over and over again."

Big Jim paused a moment releasing George's flaccid arms. "I'm restoring what you once had. I'm defeating atrophy, developing new muscle."

"A painful experience," George Williams replied. "Some nights I can't sleep."

"No pain, no gain," Big Jim recited, smiling. "Yes sir! Believe me. No pain no gain. Gotta pay your dues."

"I've already paid, George replied. "Gave my legs, my eyes, my face."

"Gotta pay the bill," Big Jim explained. "Sooner or later everyone gotta pay for being alive. Comes a time when you gotta place a bet on yourself when your future depends on what you do and if you back down from that challenge your life turns to piss water."

"Had no choice," George replied, shaking his head. "Fight or die – for God and Country."

"You still got your privates, Big Jim said. "Not everybody can say that. Count your blessings man. Count your blessings one by one."

"And fight endless wars led by men who call defeat victory – and casualties acceptable losses. What do you say about broken bodies and burned- out minds with no future and no hope?"

"I say thank God for being alive. Be grateful for the gift of life no matter how hard that life will be."

"I can't say that," George replied. "Can't deceive myself with that idea."

"There's much you can do with your life George. Like serving others less fortunate. Paying rent for being alive."

"You really believe that?"

"Yes. I also believe we're never given more than we can bear. What doesn't kill makes us stronger. We're captains of our fate if we don't quit trying. There's no such thing as a body or a soul

41

beyond repair. Look around the ward and you will see how we repair the world one broken body at a time, one broken body at a time knowing the joy of being used for a mighty purpose. You can be someone changing this fucked-up world."

A world crowded with footsteps entered his hospital room during teaching rounds, muted voices discussed lesson learned from his disability, denying him sanctuary in sleep. "Why the pity in your voices?" George Williams said. "You sent me to war so stop parading your compassion. This is a hospital not a Zoo exhibiting – genus Americanus – Habitat – USA – when not dispatched around the world to fight and die for freedom and democracy. I'm without legs, eyes and a face that's not so good to look at. Have a father and a mother and had a fiancée and a brother who never returned from his tenth mission over Germany. Death brings a sorrow that never dies, feelings that can't be discarded. Shame and disgust flood my mind like tormenting hounds of hell attacking someone unable to forget. Without forgiveness there's no redemption. No peace. Just pain.

My father dreamed the great American dream. Get rich quick. Nothing ventured nothing gained. Risked everything with a phone call to a stockbroker. Made a killing and ran to the bank and when the bank failed went bankrupt. My mother broke down. Knew nothing about stocks and bonds, how a fortune in securities became worthless overnight. My Dad never lost courage. Never jumped out his office window when the bubble burst in 1929. He just dried up and withered away. Far away.

I had other dreams. Ambitions thwarted by war. Frustrated hopes. They say the best and the brightest die young and life cuts down the most promising flowers to seed the future where they survive only in memory. I'm learning how to get in and out of bed, on and off the pot and raise a fork to my mouth without spilling food. I do sit ups, push-ups, pull-ups, abdominal crunches and weight lifts until my muscles scream with pain. They're rehabilitating my body. But what about my soul? They're teaching me how to walk, run, dance, but who will show me how to be happy with stainless steel legs and no eyes? Walking across a room without falling and getting medals is not enough to keep me from killing myself. When asked if I ever thought of suicide I said, Yes. – And asked when, – I said "this morning."

Big Jim's smile vanished, nodding as he reacted to George's admission. "Every man must find his way to his secret strength. *Why* he goes on living." Big Jim paused a moment and then resumed smiling. Speaking slowly, measuring his words. "For every man *Why* determines whether he continues living until death arrives. There's no reason to go on when we have no *Why*. You must find it for yourself."

"Where?" George asked, struggling to understand. "What are you saying?"

"I'm saying tomorrow is a good idea. Every day a fresh beginning. That's how life continues, why we come alive when looking at a child's adoring smile, embracing a woman, receiving a mother's love. There's no limit to why. Seeing sunrises and sunsets, and being able to look up at the stars and wonder what the hell it's all about is another reason why you must live."

"If you can't stand the heat get out of the kitchen," Surgeon Bob Bingham shouted at Helen, constantly criticizing her no matter how hard she tried to meet his exacting standards. Called "God" because of the many lives he saved, proud of his skill as a battlefield surgeon, Bingham was arrogant, verbally abusing assisting nurses. He intimidated anyone attempting to correct his behavior. Grieving for Ed Cronin, unhappy being reassigned to surgery, overworked, stressed, and depressed, Helen struggled to do her job despite Bingham's behavior.

"Reassign me," Helen pleaded with Ann her Nurse supervisor. "I can't work with him."

Ann, not surprised at her request, grasped Helen's hand. Shook her head. Her voice consoling. "I have no one to replace you," she replied.

"I can do nothing right," Helen said, fighting back tears.

"There's nothing's personal about his behavior," Ann explained. "He bullies everyone. He's afraid he will kill a patient with one mistake. One surgical error. If Bingham breaks down we're in big trouble."

"And so am I," Helen insisted. "I can't continue working with him."

Days and nights without food or sleep shattered Helen's composure. Bingham's rudeness overwhelmed her ability to function. Handing him instruments, counting bloody gauze pads, cleaning up catastrophic wounds without error became impossible. Sleeping pills were her salvation. Her flight from onerous duties. When awake she had long mindless conversations with herself. Calling for help. Or was it God she asked for release from her agony? There was no relief from the battle she fought with herself. No respite for her desperation. Doomed to suffer, unable to escape her misery, she descended into a long dark journey, an abyss without hope. She had no desire to awaken from a deep sleep that was neither life or death but an endless eternity. She determined not to return to the horror decimating her spirit when a familiar voice called out, repeating her name. "Please leave me be what I am, Helen replied, what I have become, a casualty of war." Then, raised to her feet, supported by Ann, they walked around the room as Ann, embracing her insisted, "wake up, wake up, this is a stupid way to die." Helen began sobbing as they continued walking, each step a journey into the future Helen refused to endure. "We'll say this never happened," Ann advised, "You did not do this." When consciousness returned, Helen remained silent. Said nothing. "I blame myself," Ann explained. "I should have reassigned you." Helen protested. Crying, "I couldn't take it anymore."

As Supervisor Ann asserted her authority training and assigning nurses to assist Doctors. She confronted Dr. Bingham insisting in her commanding voice "Helen can no longer work with you, she can't take the strain."

Removing his scrubs and mask Dr. Bingham demanded, "What are you saying? She's a good assistant. I need her."

"I'm sending Helen back to the States," Ann explained. "For R and R and reassignment."

"Why is she going home?"

"She O.D. on sleeping pills."

Dr. Bingham turned away from Ann. Remained silent. Shaking his head, he slowly walked away. "Poor girl," he said. "I'm sorry to hear that."

"You should be," Ann replied, following him. "You're were very hard on her."

Dr. Bingham stopped, turned and faced Ann. "Surgery is no tea party."

"Nurses have feelings. They can't stand being bullied," Ann insisted.

"Bullied?" Dr. Bingham asked. "Bullied? What the hell are you saying?"

"Your anger, your shouting, being impossible to please. Helen couldn't take the abuse."

Dr. Bingham enjoyed Scrub Nurses dressing him in a sterilized gown. With his face masked, head capped, hands gloved, he was a dedicated warrior prepared for battle, a Knight in armor feeling a surge of power every time a scalpel was placed in his hand. His weapon in an ongoing battle against death. Silently praying for his skill to return, he touched the blade to a patient's skin making his first incision, entering the wondrous interior of a human body. What God hath wrought with love and Man abused with war. Repairing catastrophic combat damage, tying off arteries, removing shrapnel from lungs and brains, amputating arms and legs accompanied by the rhythmic pinging of a heart monitor, Dr. Bingham concentrated on defeating an enemy unforgiving of error in a heroic fight against mortality. Every fatality a personal failure. A shameful defeat.

Recognizing the truth of Ann's description of his behavior, Dr. Bingham felt the remorse of a good man who had injured someone. His arrogance redeemed by humility, he went to the hospital where Helen was recovering. Entering her room he stood at her bedside and watched her sleep. A Penitent who had violated his oath to do no harm. Without awakening her he apologized, tears purging his soul, restoring pride, restoring self-respect.

After ninety days of R and R, re-assigned to a Stateside Hospital, Helen preferred caring for Rehab patients to nursing bloody combat casualties. After six months of Rehab, George Williams was optimistic. Happy to see Helen again.

As Helen entered his room with a lunch tray, he asked, "Teach me how to dance. I would like to learn to dance," George Williams said smiling a welcoming smile.

Setting the tray down Helen asked, "Are you serious?"

"If I can walk, why can't I dance?"

"Ask Big Jim to teach you. That's something he can do."

"I don't want to dance with Big Jim. He's not my type."

"And I am, I suppose?"

"Yes. Definitely."

Helen reached out to a small portable radio on the window ledge. Turning it on she dialed "The Make Believe Ballroom" filling the room with music. She snapped her fingers in time with the beat singing the lyrics. "You must learn to hear the rhythm," she explained. "If you can't hear the rhythm you'll never learn to dance."

"Like the beating of my heart," George said. "Your heart and mine."

Helen stopped singing and laughed. "Yes," she replied. "That's the idea. But get out of that chair, stand up and put your arms around me."

George rose from the chair and opening his arms smiled. "Like this?" he asked.

"Yes," Helen replied, hesitating a moment before entering his embrace. "Stand up, keep your head back and do what I do with my feet," she explained. "Start counting, one two three, one two three, one two three. Slow and easy, like floating on air."

George began counting, moving awkwardly on prosthetic legs.

"Yes," Helen said. "Dancing makes you feel a part of someone you love. Someone you belong to. More alive. Happy."

"Is that what you feel?" George asked.

"I don't know," Helen replied. "I don't know. Never danced with a Prosthetic before."

Yes, George is the most alive man I've ever met, Helen thought. Full of life. With the burned tissue removed George is now easier to look at, and with more skin grafts almost handsome.

"I like dancing with you," George said, interrupting Helen's thoughts.

"Reminds me of happier days, when the world was young and we were beautiful. Does my face shock you?"

"Not anymore, after debridement you're growing new skin. You're beginning to look like a movie star."

"Cary Grant? Clark Gable?"

"No. Just like someone I knew before the war," Helen replied, her voice nostalgic.

"Was he handsome?"

"No. Not handsome. Just a good face. Strong. Determined. My father said every man's face is his biography."

"And what do you see in my face?"

"Courage. Something I admire in a man."

George remained silent. Thinking of what she admitted. After a pause he asked quietly. "Helen are you falling in love with me?"

"I hope not," Helen replied. "I hope not."

The Patriot

TWO

"Saved for another day.
Saved for hunger
And wounds and heat
For slow exhaustion
And grim retreat"
For a wasted hope
And sure defeat."

Lt. Henry G. Lee USA

"No Poppa, No Mama, No Uncle Sam, we're the Battlin' Bastards of Bataan!" sang Private Edward Cronin USA marching sixty-six miles along the Philippine Island's notorious "Highway of Death." Seventy-six thousand defeated American and Filipino soldiers denied food and water, tormented by the sun, walked from the battlefield to a prison camp. Stragglers were shot. Prisoners falling on the road where they lay dying were run over and crushed by trucks and tanks. Filipinos angered by such barbarism offered food and water to the starving thirsty POW's and were bayoneted by soldiers outraged by demonstrations of sympathy for men accepting the dishonor of surrender. The Japanese believed Warriors must die in battle to be worthy of respect. But not these Americans with their arrogant belief in white supremacy. Officers using Samurai swords decapitated prisoners while lower ranks bayoneted them.

Ed Cronin walked on with hope in his heart anticipating the day when he would return to Helen's loving embrace. "No war lasts forever. I'll be free in '43" he said confidently.

Whenever he fell Ed Cronin was raised to his feet by his comrades. Held upright as he struggled to stay with the column,

49

encouraged to ignore pain, fight despair, keep moving. Wounded POW's, unable to walk, were carried on litters for a soldier never leaves another soldier behind. For four years discipline enabled them to survive hunger, wounds, illness and brutal captivity sustained by love for each other. Comradeship. A feeling surpassing what they felt for family, friends and sweethearts like Helen whose image Ed Cronin held in his mind to dispel despair. He counted footsteps as if each step brought him closer to when the war would end. He walked in a trance his mind numbed by fatigue and with other angry prisoners he chanted the derisive ballad:

"Dugout Doug MacArthur lies a shaking on the Rock" showing contempt for a General who abandoned them and fled to safety saying – "I will return" without answering the question "When? How soon?"

Ed Cronin wrote letters in his mind describing the horrors of the "Death March". Unsent letters forever embedded in his soul. "Dear Helen," he wrote, "Filipino civilians shouting "vaya con dios" set food and water on the roadside defying bayonets keeping them from prisoners. Some wept. Others cried out protesting Japanese brutality. Filipinos broke from the crowd to thank us for fighting to save their farms and villages. Parents wives and children of Filipino prisoners waiting on the roadside watched the troops straggle by searching for fathers, sons and husbands. A ten year old boy recognizing his father ran out and clung to him screaming and sobbing as a soldier dragged him away. Dear Helen, amidst this savagery I saw love. Incredible love. Brotherly love. Desperate wounded men showing devotion, loyalty, and compassion for each other. Sustaining our hope were coconut shells filled with water, rice balls stuffed with meat offered by Filipinos who were also starving. I saw the wounded and crippled carried on litters under a blazing sun by emaciated prisoners, good Samaritans who showed there is something divine, something holy in all men. Something eternal. Dear Helen, when I come home I will be a better man, husband and father for I have learned what does not kill makes us stronger.

But not everyone was their Brother's Keepers. Some crazed by thirst, desperate for a drink, fought for water at roadside artisan wells and spigots. Some refused to share their canteens determined to survive. Japanese soldiers called "buzzards squads" killed the dying where they fell throwing bodies into drainage ditches alongside the highway. They kept the column moving stabbing fifteen inch bayonets into the buttocks and backs of stragglers. They allowed no delay. No rest. Occasionally they would permit prisoners to lay face down in putrid pools of rain water to drink the contamination.

There was also laughter seeing overweight rear area Supply Officers unable to keep up with frontline troops, stumbling and falling, struggling to rise to their feet, disobeying the Japanese shouting "Speedo! Speedo! Speedo!" We were angry at their stupidity hoarding food in depots now abandoned and feeding the Japanese. Dear Helen we are marching north on the Old national Road to San Fernando where we will go to a POW camp by train. A twenty-two mile ride to Capas."

Ed Cronin was shoved into a small freight car with a hundred other prisoners shoulder to shoulder, belly to back, struggling for breath. In the crowded car the dying and the dead unable to fall, were kept standing for the three hour trip to Camp O'Donnell. Suffocating, hysterical, irrational, some prisoners fought each other for access to air. Some fainted. Filipinos lined the trackside offering food and water to starving men. Arriving at Capas, dead bodies were dragged out of the train and left to rot in the sun as the survivors marched three miles to the Camp.

47000 Filipinos and 9000 Americans were housed in two compounds and sheltered in open air barracks. To fill canteens prisoners waited in long lines at three spigots fed by one artesian well supplying water for both compounds. Hungry, thirsty, emaciated, tormented by the blazing sun, some prisoners standing in line for hours fainted while others died falling with empty canteens clutched in their lifeless hands. Defeated, silent, staring down at the ground, they were walking dead men slowly shuffling to a water spigot patiently waiting their turn. They dreamed of armies and ships liberating them in several months or years. "We'll be free in '43" said the optimists while the less hopeful replied "Momma's door in '44." Pessimists prayed "home alive in '45".

Ed Cronin acquired a friend. Someone to intimately share hopes and fears and memories of their past. Discussing families, friends and ambitions, telling what their lives were once like reminded them of what they must come home to. An undying hope that kept them alive. Prisoners enduring confinement alone, without someone to help dispel loneliness, lost hope, accepted defeat, lay down, closed their eyes and died. Lenny, the shortest soldier in the Regiment, at five feet six inches was not taller than the Japanese guards who selected tall Americans for more brutal punishment. Lenny escaped beatings with wooden batons, bayonet stabbings and being knocked down with rifle butts.

Lenny's high spirits, and unfailing good humor entertained prisoners with jokes, double-talk and naming guards Dracula, Frankenstein, and shit-for-brains. The camp's English-speaking Commanding officer, educated in California, was called "Sunshine" in response to his smiling face when addressing prisoners. Laughter was as important to survival as food and water.

When Ed Cronin, shaking and sweating, overcome by malarial fever could not leave the barracks to stand in line for the daily meal, Lenny fed and bathed him breaking the fever with cold water compresses. When the fever broke, they exchanged names and addresses of their families promising that the survivor would someday tell of how they died. A visit that would be the only memorial to their tragic lives.

There were also hours when they did not talk. Just being together met their need for companionship. For such friendship required no words in a solitude delivered from the anguish of loneliness marking their lives more deeply than romantic love. They shared food and fears, hopes and despairs, laughter and tears recognizing friendship was a sharing while loneliness was a hammer that shatters glass but hardens steel.

When Lenny lay dying of dysentery, malaria, and starvation, his body shrunken to that of a child, Ed Cronin sat at his side holding his hand, giving him water, mopping his brow, watching him struggle for breath until his heart failed and a final gasp of air rattled his throat. Ed Cronin reached out, leaned over and closed Lenny's eyes. Staring at the corpse for a moment, overwhelmed by desolation, hesitating, sobbing, he bent down and gently kissed the cheek of the friend he had lost.

One hundred ninety-six thousand American, British, Dutch and Filipino POW's were now slave laborers working in farms, factories, and coal mines replacing men sent off to war. Ed Cronin welcomed leaving Camp O'Donnell's overflowing latrines, brutal guards and starving prisoners. Anywhere else would be better than this horror, he thought. Boarding a Troop ship sailing to Japan, housed below deck in a crowded dark cargo hold, he recalled the train ride to Capas where desperate prisoners fought each other for air, light and water. Sea-sickness and dysentery added vomit, the pungent odors of urine and excrement to the suffering prisoner's endured during a three week voyage. They were living in a sea-going latrine. Travelling at night to avoid bombing and strafing, hiding in small coastal coves during daylight, the prisoners misery aborted military discipline in hysterical explosions of fury. The strong attacked the weak fighting for food and water defying officers attempting to control their insane rage. This is the end of the world, Ed Cronin thought. A breakdown of civilization. We've surrendered not only our bodies but also our souls and this damage can never be repaired. Never be repatriated to our homes and families. We have become brutal savages no better than the Japanese. God help us!

An exploding American torpedo restored order and discipline. The screaming and fighting ended as prisoners forced open hatches, climbing up out of the hold into the fresh air and sunshine and saw the guards rowing away in lifeboats. As the ship capsized a half mile off shore, eighteen hundred POW's lined up at the ship's rail, discarded their clothes and dove into the sea, swimming to a beach, holding on to each other, the strong supporting the weak, sharing lifejackets with drowning men. Strong swimmers returned to the ship several times saving lives.

Certainly Ed Cronin and these good Samaritans deserve remembering for they fulfill our need for heroes, verifying our hunger for legends. Their stories are our pride reminding us the better angels of our nature do exist. Love survives. For without love civilization dissolves into a universal confusion where man knows nothing and loves nothing. Ed Cronin now accepted pain as a condition of existence experiencing doubt and darkness as the cost of knowing he could survive. Swimming to shore he felt confident he would someday return to Helen. For he will not only endure, he will, by God's Grace, prevail.

In the dark depths of a Japanese coal Mine, working sixteen hours a day, Ed Cronin joined ten thousand American and British slave laborers undercutting a mountain, breaking black rock faces into smaller coals, loading them into carts transported to the surface in a never ending procession of misery and exhausting work. Always hungry, fed a starvation diet, Ed Cronin counted the days of his captivity considering each one bringing him closer to liberation. The horrors of enslavement were made bearable by singing as they marched to and from work, and before the evening meal of rice and fish the reassuring strong voice of Father Lawler their Chaplain led them reciting – "The Lord is my shepherd; I shall not want. He maketh me to lie down in green pastures; he leadeth me beside the still waters. He restoreth my soul; he leadeth me in the paths of righteousness for his namesake. Yea, though I walk through the valley of the shadow of death, I will fear no evil for thou art with me; thy rod and thy staff they comfort me."

The intensified brutality of the Guards and their sullen faces told Ed Cronin the Japanese knew they were losing the war. Marching from the barracks to the mine one morning, he looked up and saw contrails on the skies high overhead tracing a flight of B-29's coming to devastate Japanese cities and he felt no pity, no compassion for the innocent civilians about to die. He heard the distant rumble of a tremendous explosion, saw an enormous black cloud darken the sky, felt strong shock waves travelling fifty miles from Hiroshima to his prison camp, and he believed he would soon see Helen and hold her in his arms forever. Now, after four years, he would return to a world of revived thoughts, feelings and discoveries where hopefully he would find peace.

The next day, awakened by the roar of aircraft engines, Ed Cronin rose from his bunk, rushed from the barracks to watch planes with white stars on their wings drop canisters containing food, cigarettes, and magazines. White parachutes floated down from the sky, welcomed by cheering prisoners waving their arms and shouting and singing *God Bless America.* Ignoring orders to remain in their barracks, some starving prisoners ran to the compound and were killed by falling canisters. Despite the Chaplain's attempt to restrain them, many ignored his advice and became violently ill and died eating too much too soon. Magazines and newspapers were as welcome as food and cigarettes, bringing news of the world no prisoner could imagine: FDR, Hitler and Mussolini dead. Rosie The Riveter working in shipyards, with baseball, football and movie Stars no prisoner remembered. The America they knew and loved had changed. Would they be welcomed when they returned? Ed Cronin studied Life magazine trying to understand the strange new world. Father Lawler sat beside him and commented: "The more things change the more they remain the same. America the beautiful will still be there when you go home."

"That's not what I'm afraid of," Ed Cronin explained. "Not what's in the magazines."

"Then what troubles you?" Father Lawler asked. "After what you've experienced there's nothing you can't deal with."

"I've changed" Ed Cronin admitted. "I'm not the same man who left America four years ago."

"You're a better man now," Father Lawler replied. "Stronger. Wiser. As a prisoner you believed in your future and by God's Grace and your courage lived to see it happen."

"Helen never wrote saying she knew I was alive."

"She may have written a hundred letters the Japanese never delivered."

"In four years, without someone to love and who loves you, life can become unbearable. Why should she wait for someone who may be dead? There may be another man in her life."

Father Lawler put down a magazine, turned, and shaking his head replied. "And what if she has been faithful? Waiting for you for four years not sure you were alive? You must have faith in the power of love, Edward, because you still love her."

Ed Cronin remained silent. Paused a moment before asking "What is your future, Father. What are you returning to?"

Father Lawler smiled. "Maryknoll Seminary to recover from Malaria and get my teeth fixed. Imbibe more of the Holy Spirit and then return to the islands I love. Filipinos are good and generous and taught me about love and loyalty and devotion. They truly live in a state of Grace. Innocent souls. I would consider it a privilege to be their shepherd."

"And if they don't want you back?"

"With God's love I will manage. All men need God and I am his servant."

Swimming was a happy alternative to painful sit-ups, push-ups, leg lifts, and weight-lifting. Wheeled to the side of the pool by Big Jim, George Williams pushed down on the arms of his wheelchair and lifted his body into another chair suspended from the overhanging arm of a crane. Shouting "away we go," Big Jim cranked a winch handle swinging George Williams out over the pool lowering him into the water. "Ten laps today," Big Jim instructed. "Nice and easy. If you get winded, swim to the side of the pool and rest."

Kicking with his residual limbs, embraced by the warm water, George Williams swam from the chair, his arms reaching out pulling him towards the far end of the pool. He counted strokes, each one bringing him closer to his destination and he felt the intoxicating freedom of being buoyant and fully alive, a creature of the sea. Swimming a breast stroke, he became a graceful dolphin raising his head to swallow air as he moved through the water. He felt the strength of his arms had returned. His heart beat strong and regular. His lungs clear. What more could he ask for?

After ten laps, returning to the hoist, Big Jim lifted George Williams out of the pool lowering him into his wheelchair, no longer free and mobile, now only a wounded warrior overcoming infirmity.

One day Helen Christian wheeled George Williams to the poolside, hoisted him up and out over the pool, and lowered him into the water. He heard her dive into the pool and laughing a girlish laughter surface beside him. He swam with her, matching her movements, stroke by stroke. At the far end of the pool they turned and swam back to the hoist remaining silent, with no need for words, their swim together uniting them in a bond no longer denied. They embraced, holding each other for a long passionate moment, and then laughing, pushing George away, Helen broke free and swam off. George followed, struggling to keep up with Helen's flight from feelings they shared. They embraced again. Kissed. Their bodies pressed together in the eternal language of love.

For several days Helen avoided the Burn Ward seeking other duties diverting her attention from George Williams. New feelings overwhelmed her as she struggled to understand herself. Thinking of George Williams made her desire more embraces, more connection to the man who met her yearning for fulfillment. Possessed by emotions stronger than a romantic schoolgirl in love with a high school sweetheart, she found George Williams more compelling than the boy she remembered when thinking of Ed Cronin.

She would soon give herself to George Williams. Willingly. Hungrily. Inevitably accepting the shame of her disloyalty to Ed Cronin. Her love for George Williams was a fact. She was not confusing pity for love. His courage and determination were admirable. George Williams was now her destiny.

While rehabilitating wounded veterans, Big Jim loyally served in a Navy now recruiting two hundred thousand blacks to work as cooks, stewards or stevedores. Untrained, ordered to work faster by white officers, teams of black sailors loaded highly explosive munitions on ships making World War II's greatest home front disaster inevitable. On July 7, 1944 fifty tons of incendiary bombs, depth charges and artillery shells exploded with shock waves felt in Alameda California, 48 miles from Port Chicago on San Francisco Bay. At Boulder City, Nevada, 480 miles away, many believed an Atomic bomb had detonated. Seismographs recorded a 3.4 earthquake as a three mile high fireball rained debris over a two mile area injuring 390 civilians. 320 sailors were vaporized. 202 of them black. Medics rushed to the disaster found burying body parts in a mass grave all they were able to do. There were few survivors.

In August, at San Francisco's Alameda Naval Base, 258 black sailors demanding safer working procedures refused to load Munitions on ships supplying the war in the Pacific. 208 were Court Marshaled receiving Bad Conduct discharges and the loss of three months pay. The Mutiny's leaders, "The Port Chicago 50", were sentenced to 8 to 15 years hard labor and given dishonorable discharges. When public outrage at this injustice challenged the verdict, a second trial confirmed the initial sentence.

In 1946, the NAACP, fighting to free "The Port Chicago 50", succeeded in reducing their sentences to Bad Conduct discharges showing that litigations and demonstrations can correct injustice. The Civil Rights movement's arduous struggle to achieve liberating Supreme Court decisions now seemed inevitable. Civil Rights became a cause Big Jim would willingly sacrifice his life for. A career as demanding as rehabilitating veterans. He determined to never again passively accept discriminatory laws and humiliations.

Main Street in Hayes, Big Jim's home town, was a tarred road connecting impoverished South Carolina farmers with more prosperous coastal cities. Dogs sleeping in the middle of the highway were often killed by motorists. A General Store, Barbershop, Bank and Baptist Church met the need for food, clothing and eternal salvation. Share-cropping cotton and tobacco farms earned incomes far below standards for poverty. Every Saturday morning, arriving in pick-up trucks or horse-drawn wagons, in bib overalls and battered Stetson hats or colorful cotton dresses, farm families greeted each other while on the front porch of the General store, observing the day's events, the chronically unemployed sat on ancient rocking chairs smoking corn-cob pipes, chewing tobacco, and expectorating black juice from their bulging unshaved cheeks.

Defying 75 years since Emancipation, white citizens demonstrated their hostility towards blacks by burning thirty foot high fiery crosses on nearby hills. When their Minister called hanging a black body from a tree an un-Christian act – keeping blacks in roles assigned to them by God continued unchanged – as lynching was a public entertainment and a blood sport.

Big Jim requested and was given a 30 day compassionate leave to go to Hastings and care for his dying mother. He did not look forward to returning. Seeing the old schoolhouse and Baptist church again evoked no sentimental feeling for his home town. He was now an unwelcome intruder strolling main street in his handsome uniform and decorations. A tall, impressive challenge to social customs maintaining a segregated society. Big Jim refused to step off sidewalks into the street as whites approached. Nor would he turn his head and respond when addressed as "Boy". Big Jim was a first class Petty officer in the United States Navy and no poor white trash bigots could take that from him.

The Stars and Bars Barbecue Café, named for the Confederacy's "Grand Old Flag", was the Town's claim to fame. A renowned Truck Stop feeding patrons foods unchanged since "The War between The States." South Carolina mustard and vinegar based Barbecue was considered superior to ketchup and molasses recipes. Marinated Pork, beef and ribs created meals celebrated by tearing eyes, stomach rumblings and resounding belches.

With front doors open 24 hours a day, the Café welcomed tourists, long haul truck drivers and local patrons with a broad smile, a "howdy do", and "what can I do for you today?" A window in the rear of the restaurant served black customers who accepted segregation as an inevitable part of living and working in a southern state. Big Jim's hunger for real old fashioned barbecue was a childhood memory that could not be denied as he walked in the front door of the Stars and Bars Café and sat at the counter. Someone shouting "My God what have we here?" pulled the plug on the juke box behind the bar. Frightened by the sudden silence, the waitress turned her back on Big Jim and disappeared into the kitchen. No one spoke. Ignored for several minutes, Big Jim pushed back his chair, stood up, carefully straightened the creases in his uniform, and head high, proudly marched out of the café in a bold defiant statement.

Few Hastings' residents were surprised when Big Jim did not attend his mother's funeral. It seemed he had vanished. After 90 days, when he failed to return to duty, the Navy considered him AWOL. Absent without leave. 12 months later, they declared Big Jim a deserter and dishonorably discharged him from the United States Navy.

In Hastings, It is well-known and now part of the town's folklore, no black ever again walked through the front doors of the Stars and Bars Barbeque Café and lived to tell the tale.

One more test of Ed Cronin's resilience was the four thousand mile journey on an overloaded Troop transport sailing from Tokyo to San Francisco's Golden Gate. Three thousand combat veterans and 800 POW's crowded into cargo holds slept in short narrow bunks and were without showers or sanitary toilet facilities for nineteen days. Fed C-rations twice a day by overworked mess cooks, "home alive in forty-five" seemed a prayer come true. After surviving horrific Pacific Island invasions and liberating the Filipinos, returning soldiers, marines and prisoners fought a leisurely battle against boredom playing poker, rolling dice, or standing for hours at the ship's rail staring out to sea. Life below decks was suffocating. Fresh air intoxicating. It was good to be alive.

Why did he survive when so many friends died? Ed Cronin wondered. Why was he alive? Could his future have a higher purpose, or would he marry Helen and only live the great American dream? Watching the sun set with Father Lawler, a ritual they shared every evening, Ed Cronin turned to the Priest and said: "I can't understand so many deaths. What meaning did they have? Will their suffering be with me forever?"

Father Lawler stepped from the ship's rail and thought about Ed's question a moment before saying: "My son, God always has a purpose when sparing lives. Understanding his purpose will give your life meaning. In a world of endless savagery you must choose love instead of hate, service to others instead of selfishness."

"Easier said than done, Father," Ed Cronin replied. "Easier said than done."

"Yes," Father Lawler explained. "It's not so easy having compassion for all who suffer. For God is love and all honest thought a form of prayer. The meaning of life is a choice you make about the way you live and I have no doubt you will make the right choices with dreams that someday will come true." Ed Cronin nodded his response. Remained silent. Did not reply. Father Lawler turned and watched the setting sun glorify the evening sky. Shaking his head he closed his eyes and Ed Cronin saw tears streaming down his cheeks. Father Lawler leaned against the ship's rail gazing out to sea as if searching for God's Truth.

"We are all entitled to some happiness in our lives," he said hopefully.

The Hospital's Chaplain was not someone Helen ever wanted to see again. She recalled his sorrowful face in 1942 as he handed her a telegram stating Ed Cronin was KIA, killed in action. Standing beside him, an Army Officer, in full dress uniform, respectfully honored her loss by presenting her with a flag folded in a triangle. Three years later, when the Chaplain told Helen Ed Cronin was alive, a Prisoner of War, she wondered would she now be asked to return that heart-breaking memorial of her grief, the flag?

Recalling years of mourning, Helen wanted to scream away her anger at the blindness of fate denying her joy at this good news. Ed Cronin coming home would soon arrive at America's Golden Gate, San Francisco. Her Fiancé she had believed lost forever was now alive. And, she asked herself, what must she do when the dead rise from the grave? And what about her love for George Williams?

She had held his arm the first time he rose from bed to stand on prosthetic legs. She felt him struggling to maintain balance, head high, like an infant enjoying freedom, hesitating, fearful, summoning the strength to step forward, each new faltering step bringing tears to her eyes. She had watched him walk across the Rehab room, danced and swam with him, laughing and crying as they shared his delight in mobility. George Williams, the child she never had, now belonged to her. After so many years of love, and caring, how could she abandon him?

But what would Ed Cronin expect after his years as a prisoner? And could she live with the shame of being unfaithful? They were not the young lovers who went off to war. Life's not fair, she told herself, angrily. And happiness an impossible dream. Yes. No matter what she decided, she would hurt someone she loved.

"George Williams is only a hospital romance," Supervising Nurse Ann advised when Helen confided in her. "Real love is not a scene in a romance novel. It's hard to distance yourself from someone you bathe and shave and feed and when you start holding his hand and feel sorry for him you are lost. Fallen into an emotional abyss. No matter what Poet's say, falling in love isn't paradise but feelings that take over your life when you believe you can't live without your man."

"George Williams needs me."

"True. But what do you need Helen?"

"Not to lose George."

"By disappointing Ed Cronin?" Nurse Ann replied, "By breaking Ed's heart? By living with the guilt of having done something you will be ashamed of for the rest of your life?"

"How can love be shameful?" Helen asked.

"Because Ed Cronin will live never letting you forget, needing the woman who has betrayed his love."

"I can't help what I feel."

"I know. Many years ago I made a wrong choice. I was young, anticipating life with the man of my dreams. He went to war and when he returned he found me in someone else's arms. He had been a POW dreaming his dreams of what would happen when he came home weakened by hunger and the privations of prison. I thought he was strong enough to accept what I had done. I was wrong. He put a gun in his mouth and blew his brains out."

"How horrible."

"Yes. Horrible. Unforgivable. I was unable to love or live with any man again. No marriage. No children. No future. Two lives were lost when he pulled the trigger. Two wasted lives. Don't let this happen to you, Helen. Don't let this happen to you."

THREE

On the fifth of August, in the year 1775, the heroic Spanish navigator Captain Juan de Ayola sailed into San Francisco Bay as the first of many Europeans discovering California's beauty and harvesting its wealth. Russian Fur Traders from Alaska, New England Whalers returning from Pacific hunting grounds, and Clipper ships rounding Cape Horn brought thousands of settlers to the territory won from Mexico in 1848.

In October 1945, following other historic voyagers, the US Troopship *Invictus* steamed under the Golden Gate Bridge transporting three thousand combat soldiers and 800 POW's cheering at the ship's rail as they entered the bay. Fireboats shooting water into the air led a welcoming fleet of yachts and Tug boats, their sirens and horns rattling windows on shore. Crowds on the Presidio's beaches cheered and fired rockets into the air as an American Legion Brass Band played *God Bless America*. On the ramparts of the old Spanish Fort, a cannon thundered greetings answered by the horn of a passing Ferryboat crowded with exuberant sightseers. Inmates on Alcatraz Island looked out across the bay at the returning ship with patriotic fervor for they were also Americans celebrating a great victory.

Ed Cronin, stood at the ship's bow as they turned north into the upper bay, past Ayola cove, Sausalito, and Tiburon Island, and after completing a nineteen day voyage from Japan breathing only warm, moist, salty sea air, he now inhaled the verdant odors of wine orchards and redwood forests. In the distance he could see the snow-capped foothills of the High Sierras proclaiming the grandeur of the American continent. He was coming home alive in nineteen forty-five, an unexpected gift with daunting possibilities. And when docking at the Mare Island Naval Base Ed Cronin looked down at the crowd of expectant families he felt the fear of possible disappointment. Would Helen be there to greet him? he wondered. Did she wait for him to return? He raised his hand and waved, turning to search for a familiar face. The one in a photograph he stared at for four years trying to sustain memory of past joy. Was he expecting too much? Would Helen recognize and still love his emaciated body, eyes haunted by privation, hair grayed by brutality? A Brass Band played *Happy Days Are Here Again,* the crowd cheered as Ed Cronin walked down the gangplank and stepped ashore into the unknown of his tomorrow.

Now an avid reader of the Shipping News publication, Helen searched for the date of Ed Cronin's arrival. Agonizing weeks looking for a listing that could change her life. Nurse Ann, her supervisor, again advised Helen to keep her vows and gave her leave to travel to Mare Island Naval Base to meet Ed Cronin. Helen endured the long, hot, Greyhound Bus ride along the bay's eastern shore, staring out the window at a passing landscape of ramshackle homes and battered seaside docks thinking of her future. Of what to say. How should she behave? What would happen when she admitted her conflicted feelings? Wearing a new uniform, hair carefully combed and tucked under her white cap, Helen forced her way through the crowd to the dockside and looked up at the ship's rail searching for Ed Cronin. Fighting back tears, she waved, shouting his name, her voice overwhelmed by the Brass Band and hysterical crying voices. Cheers and wild applause greeted the first soldier ashore who kneeled and bent down to kiss the ground, then standing, he exuberantly raised his arms in a triumphant V for victory salute.

A disturbing victory for Helen welcoming Ed Cronin's return. The gates of emotional Hell were closing in on her as she struggled with questions with no easy answer. She remembered as a child hiking through a forest with her father, discovering the remains of a Fox who died attempting to flee from a trap. Helen felt sick then, and now, recalling her father explaining how the Fox fighting for freedom chewed his leg away. A desperate act, and Helen felt she also had no escape. No easy choice thinking about what to do with two men in her life. She loved both but was only in love with George Williams. Crazy in love, a kind of love with feelings she did not know she possessed, her existence enriched by a renewed hunger to live. And yes, her love for Ed

Cronin was no youthful illusion. It was not "puppy love". It was also real.

When Ed Cronin stepped ashore Helen did not recognize him, his uniform too large for an emaciated body as he turned to search for a familiar face. Ed Cronin seemed worn out, his eyes the lifeless thirty-yard stare of the combat veteran who had seen too much death and dying and chose not to see any more. Helen shouted his name and waved her arm emerging from the crowd, running towards him after assuring herself this was Ed Cronin. He turned and watched her sudden appearance, nodding and smiling opening and closing his arms around her in a sudden embrace that left him weak and trembling. Helen began crying, her tears evoking the pain and sorrow of lost years. The romantic young love that will never come again for war destroyed that possibility and hope. For Ed Cronin, coming home from war, Helen realized, she was that hope.

"Welcome home," Helen shouted, embracing Ed Cronin for the first time in four years.

Uncertain of what to answer Ed Cronin waited a moment before replying "Looks like a July Fourth without fireworks," and pointing at the waiting crowd said – "A Brass Band just for me!"

Helen laughed, now more confident, replied "You can say that again." Then, straining for words to continue the conversation — she asked – "How was the Pacific? Were you seasick?"

"Believe me the Pacific's not so Pacific," Ed confessed. "Nineteen boring days staring at the ocean wondering if you've changed."

Helen hesitated. Thought for a moment before replying "Of course I've changed. And so have you."

Ed nodded. "Well, no matter who you are now," he said, "I'm glad to see you."

"Now and forever?" Helen asked. "Now and forever?"

"I hope so," Ed Cronin replied. "But maybe that's too much to expect."

When Johnny comes marching home people shout Hurrah! Hurrah! But who are they cheering? Twenty million dead? Are we doomed to fight wars, wave flags while dancing on the rubble of our cities? We believe in life, liberty and the pursuit of happiness singing *God Bless America* where winners take all and losers sleep in doorways along our city's streets. We tolerate our insatiable lust for power and show intolerance for anyone who appears different. Will hatred and cruelty diminish our humanity and frustrate our need to live peacefully with each other?

Sedating pain does not always work. Some emotions can never be subdued. Helen's strength was forged on the battlefield and her healing touch and presence were indispensable. Patient's stopped feeling sorry for themselves when Helen entered the Burn Ward. Her high spirits and courage were contagious. Told she must do for Ed Cronin what she did for George Williams was not what Helen wanted to hear.

"Do you pity Ed?" Nurse Ann asked. "Are you trapped in a romantic illusion? Life is unforgiving and remorse painful so choose carefully, Helen, choose carefully."

Helen shook her head. A painful gesture. Resolute and determined.

"I can't do what you ask," she insisted, trembling, "I can't put aside my feelings for George and run off to take care of Ed."

Helen began sobbing, crying out: "I don't want Ed to expect something that can never happen."

A paging voice interrupted her plea, calling a doctor's name. "Romantic nonsense," Nurse Ann replied. "An adolescent dream." Helen stepped back and turned away. Angered by her unwanted advice.

"Disappointment, living without hope is dangerous," Nurse Ann continued. "Ed needs time to rebuild his life. Time to fight off drugs, or despair that could make him another casualty of war."

"We're both casualties of war," Helen insisted. "There should be a limit to what we must sacrifice."

Reluctant to inflict more pain Nurse Ann affectionately reached out to touch Helen's cheek. "You both need time to know each other. Who is Ed Cronin? Who are you? What will he do if you break his heart?"

"I'm no Saint," Helen said. "I can't help how I feel."

Nurse Ann remained silent. Restrained from questioning Helen about her future, a love story written with their lives as they descended deeper into the memory of their love for each other.

"Love grows as we enter the soul of our beloved," Nurse Ann said. "Love changes as we change, becomes intensified. Without growth, love shrivels and dies. We reach out and touch godliness when we love, restoring our faith in being alive, discovering strength that can be drawn upon when needed."

And what about love? George Williams wondered. Without eyes, legs or a face, disfigured, crippled, am I still the same man while the inner one remains a ghost haunting my dreams where I walk, see, make love, and look handsome again?

In my dreams I run free as a floating cloud racing towards the finish line, spectators cheering as I plunge through the tape, the Band playing *The Star Spangled Banner* as I embrace Helen. Do I have the right to hold on to her like a drowning man struggling to take one more breath, one more grasping of the golden threads of love binding a man and woman together forever?

Ed Cronin learned what Christianity was all about watching Father Lawler serve as prison camp Chaplain. Giving Last Rites, comforting the distraught, encouraging men without hope, this modest Brooklyn Irishman, never seemed to eat or sleep. With astounding energy he provided moral and spiritual guidance sustaining their belief in survival. Colonel Mitsui, the Camp's Commandant, who wouldn't execute a prisoner without first praying to his Shinto God, respected Father Lawler's religiosity often conferring with him about running the camp.

An extraordinary man living an extraordinary life, Father Lawler evoked Ed Cronin's memories of his frequently unemployed alcoholic father and saintly mother raising six children on her husband's irregular pay. Housed in cold-water flats, enduring repeated evictions, the Cronins struggled to find a place to live. Ed Cronin wondered would he, like his father, die a broken man, a warm meal in a church basement all he could look forward to nodding and dreaming of his childhood in Ireland. Ed Cronin determined to have a better life than loading cargo, stealing from broken crates raised from the dark bowels of a Freighter and then dropped to the dock to break open like Manna from heaven.

After six months Survivor's Rehab, Ed Cronin visited New York's "Hell's Kitchen" where he recalled childhood days diving into the Hudson river, swimming under piers to escape blistering summer heat. He returned to his father's neighborhood of loan sharks and corrupt Dock bosses where crowded Bars provided a home away from home for Dock Workers. With sawdust on floors bowls of pigs knuckles on the bar, and photographs of baseball and football stars on the walls, his Father's sanctuary from work was somehow now different. Absent were loud whiskey-soaked voices of angry men now quietly listening to a tall, thin Priest drinking boiler-makers with them. Speaking in an Irish brogue the Priest explained his mission. "The docks are my church and if you don't think Christ is down here on the waterfront you have another guess coming." The Priest paused a moment, his voice rising as he explained in a sonorous voice "Christ is here in the daily shape-up redeeming all men."

"What are you saying?" Ed Cronin asked. "What do you want?"

Father Corridan opened his arms as if embracing his congregation. "I want more!" he insisted. "I want more food! More clothing! Better housing! A greater share of what men earn by the sweat of their brow!"

A Dock worker applauded. "Say that again Father!" he shouted, nodding agreement. "That's a God-given truth!"

After another Beer and whiskey chaser the Priest cleared his throat. "The waterfront is a jungle where there are too few jobs for too many men. We must abolish the Shape-up. Scrambling for work tokens thrown on the ground is demeaning."

"That's how it's always been," Ed Cronin responded. "That's what these men accept."

"Sad but true," Father Corridan answered. "For generations they tipped their hats and bowed to their superiors. Held down so long they've forgotten what it is to stand and demand their rights. They must learn they are brothers, not savages fighting for jobs, waiting for those moments when whiskey resurrects their courage. Restore their self-respect and they will lose their subservience."

"How is that possible?" Ed Cronin asked.

"Show them they can be free of exploitation and they will choose a decent life instead of a living death."

"My father never had a chance to make that choice."

"And my father worked a twelve hour day for a dollar and was grateful for the job. That must change."

"And how do you do that?"

"Teach dock workers they are men and not cattle ruled by criminals exploiting their ignorance."

"I've seen the best and worst in man," Ed Cronin replied. "As prisoners they can be mean and selfish. They fight for food you wouldn't feed to a dog, or kill for a breath of fresh air. They will also, without hesitating, dive into the sea to save a drowning shipmate."

"That's why we should never stop trying to change man. Everyone can become that little spark of humanity that makes justice possible."

Ed Cronin turned from the Priest, finished his drink, and walked out of the Bar. He had heard more than he could understand. A Priest preaching and drinking with Parishioners was remarkable.

On the river, a Tug Boat towed a Freighter from the dock sounding a mournful horn echoing Ed Cronin's feelings. Maybe it's true, he wondered, the waterfront is Calvary where men die trying to feed their families. Change is possible if dock workers fight to make it happen. He walked to the end of the pier and stared down at the river flowing out to sea on an ebb tide. Perhaps here on the docks I will find what I'm searching for, Ed Cronin wondered as he reached down and picked up a small white stone. Holding the stone in his hand he studied its pristine beauty so incongruous on the waterfront. Raising his arm, with a sudden surge of strength Ed Cronin threw the stone far out into the river accompanied by the cries of seagulls.

Dear Edward,

I wrote many letters you never received during our troubled years of uncertainty. The report you were missing raised my hopes you were alive and I continued believing someday you will come home to me. Only when you were reported dead did I stop writing, and drowning in my grief, I refused to accept losing you and our dream of a happy life together. Now my joy at your return is troubled by questioning your expectations of me. What are they? And can I meet them? The war has changed who we are though my love for you is as strong as ever and I hope you feel the same about me.

While you were a prisoner something happened beyond my control. I fell deeply and truly in love with someone I cared for as a nurse in the burn ward. His name is George Williams and I held his hand the first time he rose from bed to stand on prosthetic legs. A heroic effort that touched my heart. I watched him struggle to maintain balance, head held high, hesitating, fearful, each step bringing tears to my eyes as he walked across the rehab room. It was like watching a child learning to walk and I felt this man must forever be a part of my life.

This love was different, more compelling from what we felt for each other four years ago. With George Williams I felt a beautiful tragic tenderness, a longing to become a part of another person yet remain more myself than ever before. I felt a doubling of the experience of life and love that comes from believing the two of us were one. The sweet union of our bodies and the wonders of the human heart healed old wounds binding us in the golden threads of love that nothing and no one can ever tear apart. Yes, my love for you will remain alive as long as we live, and I hope you find in your heart understanding of what is in mine. What I feel for you and for George Williams is a blessing, not a tragic curse as long as we continue to believe in the healing power of love.

Love, always.
Helen

A poem for Helen

My songs will vanish in the night
My heart is emptied of its fright
An empty heart cannot sing
Not knowing what love can bring.

Dear Helen,

I now know what pain love can bring, and I thank you for your honest letter for without truth the chemistry binding two people together cannot work it's magic. I believe sharing happiness and sorrow with another person is the greatest choice we make in life. Recognizing the beauty of the one we love makes an enduring marriage possible for we can never fully know each other and the difficulties of being in love always hurt. When wounded, we grow apart learning it is better to have loved and lost than not to have loved at all.

Our feelings for each other are still with us at this moment in our lives. The memory of our love will never vanish from who and what we are, sustaining us in whatever course our lives may take. I don't feel I have lost you. Our continuing thoughts of each other will be as binding as any marriage vows. While we travel separate paths to happiness we will never be alone. For true love is eternal.

Love always,
Edward

George Williams began each day determined to make the most of his resurrected life by struggling to rise from bed and walk on prosthetic legs. Reaching out to grasp a helpful hand he identified visitors by their voices and footsteps. Sound became sight, overcoming blindness, making him wonder could he now have a life worth living being less of a man than he once was? He had suffered and survived the moral injury affecting combat survivors until in despair some blow their brains out to escape the shame and remorse haunting their lives. His first personal victory over malignant fate was walking a thousand yards from the Burn Ward to the far end of the hospital corridor. With each step the hallway became an avenue of healing. A Sanctuary.

Writing became his refuge dictating words for everyone to read. Writing met his need to tell all he experienced for what was his injured body but the container of his mind and spirit? Living by and for writing would become the central activity of his life making him more than one who merely exists and dies forgotten and unknown, without conscious knowledge of who he was.

George Williams wrote about flying over Tarawa Atoll at five thousand feet above an Armada of 80 warships and 35000 Marines determined to defeat 4700 Japanese on Betio island. Flying protective air cover over the Pacific War's largest beach landing, George Williams looked down at a Naval Task Force advancing beneath a peaceful tropical sky of slowly drifting cumulus clouds. He saw shrieking 16 inch shells exploding in bursts of orange flame devastating Bomb shelters and artillery emplacements on shore. Rising from the rubble, towering pillars of black smoke concealed George Williams' assigned targets and not until the smoke cleared did he lead a flight of Hellcats bombing and strafing the blood – stained coral sands of this island fortress.

In Naval War College games Admiral Harry Hill, Commanding this Task Force, had studied all the tactical and strategic plans needed for victory. Attacking at dawn, at low tide, a fleet of Landing Craft departed from Troop ships and waited offshore for their turn to proceed to the beach. Rolling in the ocean swells, sea-sick, the first, second and third waves would follow each other in a scenario based on the best available Weather and Oceanographic intelligence.

But as a Poet observed – "the best laid plans – oft go astray." Dismissing prior warnings from his staff, Admiral Hill minimized the hazard of a Neap tide. One that comes just after the first or third quarter of the moon where there is least difference between high or low water grounding all boats by the failure of the ocean to rise.

On this day the ocean just sat there at a three foot depth grounding Landing raft on the coral reef surrounding the island. The first wave ran aground six hundred yards from shore as George Williams dove down to strafe the beach, giving protective air cover to the Marines wading ashore waist deep in water, their legs bloodied by razor sharp coral. Defenseless against Japanese machine guns, one third were casualties. The second and third waves followed, were grounded, wading ashore to seek shelter behind a seawall on the beach where they dug in trapped between the sea and the Japanese.

Ammunition exhausted, his guns silent, George Williams returned to his Carrier thinking: "Theirs not to reason why, theirs but to do or die." In three days, after several more tragic beach landings, the Japanese were defeated with a loss of 3000 Marines sacrificed because their Commander had blundered.

Sickened by this waste of lives, George Williams raged against the folly and pity of war. Is every generation doomed to devour the best and brightest of its young? he asked himself. Are we to continue killing in recurring wars incapable of changing our fate? Believing in Duty, Honor, Country, have we become captive to forces beyond our control? Can I no longer be true to myself knowing going to war blood-stains my soul? Is dying for my country heroic?

George Williams wrote about his friend Max Schumacher who spoke with a courteous southern drawl women found attractive. Keeping apart from the Squadron's light-hearted camaraderie, Max showed the strain of too many deployments suffering stress alcohol could not relieve. George Williams wondered how much more can Max endure before breaking down? What are the limits of his resilience?

Rated one of the best pilots in the squadron, Max Schumacher spent his off-hours reading and writing letters. Medium height, dark hair cut short, a winning smile, he preferred studying

Intelligence Briefs to playing poker or singing and laughing and joking to relieve the tension of anticipating combat. He rarely joined his shipmates singing – "The bells of Hell go ding-aling-aling for you but not for me! Oh Death where is thy sting-aling-aling the grave thy misery?" preferring "Show me the way to go home" sung in his strong tenor voice with great feeling. He displayed none of a Pilot's death-defying swagger celebrated in films. George Williams worried about Max's ability to survive. In a real war there are no Supermen.

"I'm OK" Max Schumacher replied when George intruded upon one of his frequent episodes of depressed silence. "I'm doing fine," he said, forcing an unconvincing smile.

"You think too much," George Williams insisted. "Thinking will drive you out of your skull."

Max Schumacher nodded agreement. "It's the god damn heat and noise that gets me. What I need is more sleep."

"Maybe Doc can help you," George Williams advised.

"I don't do pills," Max Schumacher replied, turning away, retreating into silence.

George Williams observed some men show their fate in a gesture, a troubled look, their eyes revealing an apprehension of the future. Was Max one? And what could George Williams do to alter what's been ordained by the ruthless God of war?

The ship's bell tolled the hour. A voice on the P.A. system read the Orders of the Day. Overhead a catapult launched a plane into the air drowning out thought and speech.

"The Skipper's going to ground you if you don't get your shit together," George Williams said.

"I can hack it, if that's what's worrying you."

"You're a threat to everyone in your flight when you're not sharp."

"I won't let them down."

"I hope so. Get some sleep and stop crying in your beer – It's going to be a long war."

Days and weeks at sea searching for the enemy tests man's spirit and endurance. Debriefings after every mission analyze after action reports for lessons learned. When Max Schumacher's Flight returned to the Carrier missing one plane, his wingman reported being attacked by enemy fighters forming a defensive circle protecting each other's vulnerable tail. The Flight continued circling until shielded by clouds they dove away to live and fight another day. Then, to everyone's surprise, without a word of explanation or farewell, Max Schumacher broke out of the formation diving down to attack a Japanese cruiser emerging from under a protective cover of dark rain clouds. When the skies cleared his shipmates saw the wreckage of Max Schumacher's plane scattered on the burning deck of a Japanese Cruiser in a sacrifice no After Action Report could ever adequately explain.

Reacting to his friend's death, George Williams wrote in his diary – "War is a terrible thing we accept believing it unifies our country. We fight to revive our pride through violence that makes us feel good. Not understanding other cultures we devastate them with our power. Trapped between the myth of preventative violence and the cruel truth of war, we lack the courage and imagination to change a fate determined by patriotism."

On August 15th, 1943 the largest amphibious invasion force of the War approached Kiska Island with thirty five thousand troops escorted by three Battleships, two Cruisers, nineteen Destroyers, five Troop Transports, twenty cargo ships and ninety beach landing craft. Flying protective air cover over this Armada George Williams looked down at a ten mile procession of ships steaming across a frigid Arctic sea. Commanded by Admiral Thomas C. Kinkaid this well-planned attack would attempt to regain the only American territory occupied by the Japanese. Kiska Island.

Pilots overflying the Island reported no anti-aircraft fire or evidence the Japanese remained on Kiska. Despite more intelligence confirming this, Admiral Kinkaid proceeded as planned considering the attack a Training Exercise that will be of great value for future landings. Uncertain about the Japanese presence, American and Canadian troops fought for eight days against an nonexistent enemy on a fog-shrouded island suffering 24 dead from friendly fire, four from Booby traps, 71 from mines, and 168 wounded or incapacitated by Trench foot.

Approaching Kiska in a dense fog, landing craft wandered off shore at low tide grounding on unmarked reefs and rocks. Debarking on the beach the troops believed the Japanese had withdrawn into the hills and valleys overlooking the landings, ghosts made ominous by their silence. The slightest movement or noise in the fog initiated fire-fights from panicked troops firing into the mists concealing an unseen enemy. The troops dug-in seeking protection in fox holes, praying for the skies to clear allowing them to advance into the interior of the island to confront the Japanese. The persistent fog also thwarted George Williams attempt to support the landing by strafing the beaches.

After eight days fighting ghosts with no great victory possible, Admiral Thomas C. Kinkaid, convinced by new intelligence confirming there were no Japanese on Kiska, having evacuated their troops three weeks before the landing, ordered all American and Canadian forces to withdraw to live to fight another day on other Pacific islands.

"SNAFU – Situation Normal All Fucked Up!" was the sardonic assessment of the Tarawa beach landing where the forecast of an abnormal tide was dismissed by over confident leadership. "FUBAR – Fucked Up Beyond All Recognition" described attacking an abandoned Aleutian island because the commanding officer dismissed accurate intelligence. Yet despite leadership arrogance and the blinding fog of war, the nobility of brave men dying for a cause greater than themselves was a stirring sight. Despite the glory of fighting for God and Country, George Williams believed the waste of life an obscenity. "They have made a desert and called it peace" an ancient historian asked. Does war produce more evil than good when wounded Veterans bring back the war with them? George Williams wondered.

George Williams wrote in his diary: "Men do not die well who die in battle. Some are instantly killed by grenades and shells, bullets and flames, while the wounded live long enough to feel life ebbing as they gasp for breath, choking as their lungs fill with blood. There are no heroes in body bags. Only the human refuse of war where men fight and die for their beliefs. Believing their deaths are not in vain, they are convinced their country's future can be defended by killing. The curse of mankind. The pity of war."

George Williams favorite poet, Wilfred Owen, witnessing the carnage of the first World War wrote:

"My friend, you would not write with such high zest
To children ardent for some desperate glory

The old lie: Dulce et decorum est Pro patria mori."
George Williams agreed –
   it is not sweet to die for one's country.

Ed Cronin enjoyed strolling the docks watching cranes lower cargo nets into ships. Tug boat fog horns tooting at Ferry boats crossing the river revived childhood memories of the waterfront he was born into and could not forget. On a familiar street corner Old Tom's food cart still sold hot dogs, pork sausages and sauerkraut lunches for a dollar. Loan Sharks, number runners and prostitutes solicited customers while at traffic lights homeless drifters wiped windshields for twenty-five cent handouts. Teen-agers still played stick-ball under the EL as neighborhood Bars opened before noon to enable alcoholics to begin another day drinking.

Also unchanged in New York's "Hell's Kitchen" were daily "Shape ups" with Dock Bosses hiring Stevedores who kicked-back a part of their pay while the unemployed fought each other for brass job tokens thrown on the ground in an obscene struggle to earn a day's pay.

Feeling the outrage he felt as a prisoner of war watching the humiliation of desperate men, Ed Cronin was repelled. What once he accepted as normal working on the waterfront now seemed an obscenity. The reason why Dock Workers die young from alcohol and despair. His father's cruel fate.

Reviving these memories he stopped at Old Tom's food cart and handed him a dollar.

Shaking his head Old Tom raised his hand refusing payment. Staring at Ed Cronin, studying his face, he opened his arms to hug him. "You're your father's son, I can see that," he shouted, "and I thought you was dead in the war."

"Don't believe everything you hear Tom."

"Went to a memorial Mass for you dear Ed. Prayed for your immortal soul I did."

"Your prayers were answered," Ed Cronin replied.

"We were sad when your father died of a broken heart and your mother soon followed to the Hereafter." Old Tom stepped back and looked at Ed Cronin. "Hope you've not come here to shape up. This is no place for a young man back from the war. No place at all. Still the kitchen of Hell with the same devils working good men to death while robbing them blind. Kickbacks, shakedowns and murder for anyone not deaf and dumb. I tell you – stay away from the docks Ed Cronin, though I'm glad to see you looking so like your old man."

"I'm thinking of working with Father Corridan," Ed Cronin explained.

"Going to his school?" Old Tom asked.

"Yes," Ed Cronin replied. "Heard him speak, like what he's teaching."

"Do you now?" Old Tom asked. "Do you believe what has always been can be changed?"

"I'm willing to try."

"You're gonna teach men who have been down all their lives to stand up and fight for their rights with an honest Union?"

"Yes."

"Father Corridan's beautiful pipe dream," Old Tom exclaimed, shaking his head.

"It's no dream if enough men believe it."

"You can't just go from what is, to what ought to be. Love and kindness is for Saints."

"Well maybe that's who we are. Maybe there's a bit of Saint in every man."

"Yes, I know. That's what the Nuns taught us. They never worked the docks or busted their backs for starvation wages. Never watched their wives and kids die from TB and pneumonia. Never been kicked out into the street when they couldn't pay the rent. The real world ain't what they say it is. And that's the God-given truth!"

"There's other truths."

"Like what?"

"Like one man can make a difference teaching faith, hope and love, what Christianity is all about. Where justice, freedom and peace is possible for struggling, sinful suffering men. Fighting the corruption running the docks, Father Corridan is trying to change this horror."

"And not getting very far if you ask me," Old Tom replied. "The Union and the Mob and not Christ rule the waterfront. The shipping companies get their slave labor, the politicians are paid off, and all that keeps Father Corridan alive is his clerical collar."

"And his faith in Man. His belief given a chance we can do better."

"Not if the powers that be have their way. Father Corridan is fighting a battle he can't win. Crime will be with us always no matter what he preaches. His days on the waterfront are numbered if you ask me. Men like this good Priest come and go like the tide. No matter how high they rise they always fall. That's the way it is, dear Ed. I don't want you throwing your life away on a fool's errand."

The Xavier Labor School occupied an old Parish building on Manhattan's west 16th street offering a curriculum dedicated to the proposition that Christ can be found in every worker, and there is a moral connection between the church, the rights of workers, and economic justice. Combining the spiritual and the practical, the ideal and the real, Father John Corridan, seeking to establish the reign of God on earth, taught labor law, bargaining and arbitration skills, speech and ethics to uneducated dock workers in an never ending battle for social justice. He believed work is the way we worship and service to others the path to redemption.

Dismissing Old Tom's advice Ed Cronin walked down west 16th street drawn to the Xavier school by Father Corridan's preaching. Fighting the good fight for Jobs, pensions, self-respect and human dignity was a cause Ed Cronin determined to dedicate his life to.

Returning to the streets of his childhood, Ed Cronin felt dismayed walking past homeless veterans sleeping in doorways. Forgotten warriors who served their country and now stood in line at a Shelter door waiting for a bowl of soup. There was something very wrong about a society accepting social decay as normal. Certainly fighting this moral failure is doing God's work on earth.

Ed Cronin never refused Panhandlers holding out their hands for coins. They were not ghosts haunting pedestrians but living human beings worthy of respect and not shame, overcome by despair, helplessness, and a belief nothing can be changed. They were "walking wounded" injured by violence, alcoholism, and verbal abuse living out their lives where cynicism displaced faith and family love was only a memory. For what purpose do they go on living? And were they responsible for their poverty?

In 1863, a thousand draft rioters attempting to torch the city were incarcerated in the District of Columbia's red brick jail. In 1865, on a scaffold in the prison's yard, Lincoln's assassins were executed. In 1920, Immigrant "Reds" were rounded up and held before deportation by Attorney General Palmer defending our nation from communism. And in this historic site from 1917 to 1923, socialist presidential candidate Eugene V. Debbs became our nation's first political prisoner convicted of obstructing the draft. For each generation, history has been a recurring narrative of ignorance, prejudice and destructive illusions defiantly expecting a different result. The psychiatric definition of insanity.

Arrested in 1946 for organizing anti-war demonstrations, George Williams was held in a windowless cell furnished with a sleeping pad and a squat toilet. Joining other Veterans advocating repeal of the draft law, George Williams, marching on prosthetic legs, led a parade of disabled veterans down Pennsylvania avenue shouting "I have seen war and I hate war." Addressing several thousand demonstrators on the Capitol steps he aroused hopes that peace was possible through disarmament. "Going to war was not something we had to do," George Williams insisted – "violence is as American as apple pie and wars debase and corrupt our nation."

For speaking his mind George Williams was clubbed to the ground, beaten and arrested.

Before being sentenced, George Williams addressed the Court:

"Your Honor, I ask no mercy, plead no immunity, believing Truth will someday prevail. The lies we tell about war kill millions every generation, and only when we recognize war destroys more than it protects, will war lose its attraction. The savage truth of war is undeniable. We are war's victims, never triumphant Victors. Nations great and small rise and fall in recurring conflicts now made more deadly by nuclear weapons. Saying 'Hell No – We won't go' affirms our ability to save the world from mutual destruction. One world or none is not an idealistic dream but a choice we must make if we are to survive before going to war becomes tolerable and perpetual – violence to be managed rather than ended.

We are now engaged in an undeclared war on the Rule of Law and the essential values of our democracy. In the name of Patriotism too many citizens accept such governmental aberrations as – Preventative detention – wiretapping – extra-judicial murder – and No Knock entry. The War on Communism becomes a War on Dissent threatening the survival of who and what we are as the land of the free and the home of the brave. Our war on dissent becomes a war on democracy when you criminalize – undermine – subvert freedom of speech by violently attacking and jailing Protestors employing informers and using entrapment by government agents who violate the Law – to maintain Law and Order."

The Visitors Center was furnished with a long oak table and a wire mesh screen separating prisoners from friends and family. High on the back wall, through an unwashed window, a shaft of light penetrated the room's shadows where anguished voices shared their pain. Helen, in her spotless white uniform, blonde hair tucked under her white cap, reached out and pressed her palm against the screen. George Williams raised his hand and touched her fingertips in their only permissible physical contact.

"What are you doing in here?" Helen asked. Her eyes tearing. "How can you be so reckless? After all we've been through, you could have been killed."

"What are you doing out there?" George Williams replied. "Why aren't you in here with me protesting?"

"There are other ways of getting what you want," Helen insisted. "Better than being beaten and arrested."

"No more war, Helen. No more war," George Williams replied. "Don't you think that's worth fighting for?"

"A futile dream," Helen said, shaking her head. "There will always be wars and more killing and more wounded for me to take care of, for war gives meaning to men's lives."

George Williams withdrew his hand from the screen. He paused a moment before explaining:

"For years I've asked myself what am I going to do when this war ends? What will my life be? Does surviving justify my existence? Why am I alive when so many good men died? What will I be remembered for when I am gone? Who will remember me?"

"I will," Helen replied. "I will never forget you."

Helen often felt she was caring for a parade of despairing patients silently watching her as she entered the Burn ward on her morning rounds. The wounded were spectators, her daily visit most welcome. Responding to their requests, changing dressings, taking pulses and temperatures, Helen believed she was a Sister of Mercy graciously relieving pain with sedatives. Smiling, calling patients by their names, holding their hands seemed as therapeutic as a surgeon's scalpel and seeing young soldiers fighting for their lives aroused Helen's maternal instincts. She discovered she had a secret strength – the tenderness of touching another person, the healing power of her once wounded hands. Sensitive hands, with long tapered fingers and a small narrow palm that had grown new skin after being badly burned as a child. She identified objects in a dark room by touching them, and whenever she touched herself, she smiled, feeling alive and well.

Rude, arrogant doctors expecting nurses to meet their demands diminished Helen's pride and joy nursing. Doctor Bingham's abuse taught her what doesn't kill made her stronger. She now easily tolerated unreasonable criticisms, harsh, inconsiderate voices were only an unpleasant part of her job. "Campaign Wives", Nurses becoming intimate with doctors, she believed violated their oath to do no harm. Faithful to George Williams, Helen refused to party with the hospital staff ignoring their flirtations and drinking. She had looked into her heart and discovered the cause of her pain – her feelings for Ed Cronin who she disappointed evoking guilt and self-flagellation that defied forgiveness, and, if not subdued, begat self-pity. But what about compassion for herself? She had done no wrong. During the war her life had been swept along by the inexorable river of time in which each moment was a challenge. And, she had no doubt, time does not heal all wounds. Some are beyond repair becoming crippling dreams.

The roving hands of Doctors could not be ignored as they touched her arms, back, and posterior in unwanted familiarity. A violation of her dignity, for she was not a sexual object to be caressed whenever some man felt the impulse. Outraged, unable to control her anger, with silent fury, Helen reached out and slapped the surprised face of a Surgeon who patted her backside in what he thought was a friendly gesture. Helen remained silent, continued working, and, as her anger subsided, she laughed, celebrating her response to vulgarity. She refused to accept the way things were always done, believing herself any man's equal. Now more assertive, Helen felt her love for George Williams intensifying. They would grow old together; and falling madly in love again she would express her tender feelings in a connection enabling them to discover each other by ecstatically embracing.

Striking a superior officer was a severally punished Court Martial offense. The presiding officer of the Court, a Judge Advocate, secretly approving Helen's behavior, and considering the stress of Helen's duties and service, would dismiss the charge of insubordination prejudicial to good order and discipline if Helen apologized. Ending the Inquiry with an apology would prevent embarrassing publicity. Helen and the officer would shake hands, have a drink together, and no record of the event would be retained.

It's a man's world, Helen thought, refusing to apologize. As the injured party she deserved an apology and should not be asked to give one. She thanked the Judge Advocate for his offer but refused to accept more humiliation, more injustice. She was not the only Nurse enduring disrespect from Doctors. After years of indignity there came a moment when she could not take more abuse. A Court Martial would enable her to defend herself, and advocating for other Nurses, correct what is unacceptable.

The Judge was not amused. "Military Law is quite clear," he explained. "And you violated that law. You have committed a crime and it is my duty to enforce the law. Insisting on a Court Martial risks a prison sentence of several years. Not a wise choice."

The majesty of the Law be damned, Helen thought. Military law serves good order and discipline first, and justice last. A General slaps a hysterical soldier and goes unpunished while they Court Martial and execute a seventeen year old for cowardice. Many officers – "ninety day wonders" building military careers are despised by the men they command. There is the right way, the wrong way, and the army way of doing everything. CYA. Cover your ass; never hurry, never worry, never volunteer, keep your eyes open, mouth shut, and make ten copies of everything is how you do your time in the army. And yes, there are heroes; unarmed battlefield Medics under fire giving plasma to the wounded, bloodstained exhausted Surgeons cutting and probing and sewing up shattered bodies, overworked Nurses fainting from fatigue, and casualties crying for their mothers or stoically accepting the possibility of death. Yes, there are heroes, soldiers dying for their comrades, fighting for a nation unworthy of their sacrifice.

I'm no hero and have had enough of this war, Helen believed. Not getting any younger. Exhausted, with moments when I'm staring off at nothing, my mind thoughtless, out of touch with the world. I'm one of the walking wounded without relief from the horrors of seeing broken bodies. If convicted, what will I do without what gives my life meaning doing what I love? I've witnessed shining through war's agonies, the inherent goodness of man. There certainly must be a God within us singing our personal songs of existence, creating and defining who we are. Because of faith, hope, and love we become more than a speck of dirt on this planet waiting for the mushroom cloud to arrive. Working with love prolongs our lives, defeating fear and anxiety. We are no longer blind to what is constructive and beautiful. We are no longer blind to love.

"You must apologize," Nurse Ann, her supervisor advised, holding Helen's hand. "You can't beat the system. Requesting a Court Martial is a losing game. You can't slap an officer no matter how stupid they behave."

Helen shook her head. Paused a moment before replying : "A formal hearing is a risk I must take. A challenge I can't run from."

Nurse Ann, her voice more insistent replied – "Dishonorably discharged you'll never work as a Nurse again. Your life will be ruined."

Helen turned and walked away from Ann, ending the conversation. Then, reconsidering, she stopped, turned and faced her friend before answering in a determined voice. "Perhaps. Maybe," Helen said, her voice rising. "Nothing will ever change if we don't work together and do something about how we are treated."

"Work together?" Nurse Ann asked, startled by Helen's reply.

"Yes. Together we can stop this abuse," Helen insisted.

"Work together?" Nurse Ann repeated. "You're talking about a strike?"

"Yes," Helen replied. "Yes. A strike."

"Do you know what a strike is called in the Military?"

"No."

"Mutiny!"

Strolling "Hell's Kitchen's" crowded streets, Ed Cronin thought about millions dying in Ireland's "Great Famine" driving survivors across the stormy Atlantic to find a better life on the other side of the ocean. If the walls of New York's brick and wooden tenements could talk, what stories they would tell of immigrant hunger, despair and poverty. He recalled his father returning from unloading ten tons of iron ore in 150 pound canvas bags, climbing up from a ship's dark and forbidding hold where many men fell down and died from exhaustion. Certainly, Ed Cronin believed, there should be more to life than the misery endured by people convinced poverty was their God-given fate. As a prisoner of war he often thought of these crowded streets as home, and now, seeing children playing in the gutters, escaping the torrid summer heat, splashing in the cooling spray of open hydrants, he recalled a Filipino soldier saying – "the Pencil of God has no eraser. What has been, will always be. Nothing changes. From the cradle to the grave, misfortune is in the air we breathe."

An organ grinder on the sidewalk standing tall and proud cranked *My Wild Irish Rose* singing in a strong tenor voice, nodding thanks for the coins dropped into a hat at his feet. A Policeman stopped and listened, smiling nostalgically before continuing to patrol his beat. Housewives leaned out tenement windows looking down at the sidewalk to watch pushcart merchants selling their goods. It was all familiar. The noise, the crowds, the plaintive cries of "Old Clothes" buyers mingling with the clop clop clop of horse drawn wagons fouling the streets. These were his people, and here he would live, and walking to the river to the docks, he stopped and stared at the face of a Stevedore drawn on a wall. "Where is Tommy Gleason?" a question written beneath the portrait said. And walking further down the street to the corner, Ed Cronin saw attached to a lamp post, a cardboard poster asking – "Where is Tommy Gleason?"

Stopping at Old Tom's Cart and refusing a welcoming offer of food, Ed Cronin asked: "Who the hell is Tommy Gleason?"

Old Tom remained silent as if refusing to answer a painful question.

"Who is he?" Ed Cronin demanded. "Who is Tommy Gleason?"

"A Martyr," Old Tom replied in a sorrowful voice. "If ever there was one, Tommy Gleason is a Martyr who one day just disappeared. Hasn't been seen for almost a year now. Some say he's in the bottom of the Hudson wearing concrete shoes. Them posters are like stations of the cross put up so we remember what he died for. Went to Father Corridan's Labor school, he did. Learned to organize dock workers and was killed trying to charter an honest Union and abolish the Shape Up. Tommy and Father Corridan fought the powers that be and lost, as everyone said they would. After the men returned to work, after the strike, the Owners hired two hundred Convicts paroled from prison to enforce the kick backing, loan sharking and numbers game run by Joe Ryan's Pistol Local. The Cons fought a bloody battle to prevent having a Hiring Hall where men got work on seniority, time in the hold and ability. Broke a lot of heads and legs, they did, and Tommy's not the only Dock Worker coming to his eternal rest in the bottom of the Hudson."

"Who killed him?"

Old Tom shook his head. Laughed. "No one knows. On the waterfront everyone's D and D, Deaf and Dumb. Say anything and you'll never work again. That is, if they don't kill you like in the old Murder incorporated days when a contract cost fifty dollars."

"So nothing's changed during the war."

"Everything was worse. You couldn't go out on strike during the war. It wasn't patriotic. And when the fighting stopped, and Tommy and Father Corridon got 30,000 Dock Workers to shut down 118 piers for 25 Days, all they got for their courage was a fact-finding Commission to hear their grievances. The Chairman was a Shipping executive who found nothing wrong on the waterfront. So there were a lot of hungry children during the strike. Families couldn't buy food. Pay the rent. Stay warm. A lot of suffering that changed nothing."

"So why keep asking about Tommy Gleason?"

"Many believe he is alive and well and will return someday and organize another strike. Paint his face on a wall, nail up a poster, keep asking about him, and it's like he's still alive. He ain't dead. That is to say, what he fought for ain't dead. Tommy's still with us fighting for a Hiring Hall instead of the shape up. It seems some men and their ideas never die. What they fought for lives long after they are gone. They become like Saints keeping up our hope that change is possible. I guess you might say Tommy Gleason lives in the heart of every dock worker who ever dreamed of a better life for his children."

On July fourth 1946, George Williams led two thousand disabled veterans down Pennsylvania avenue chanting – "No More War! No More War!"' Walking wounded of world war two demanding repeal of the draft paraded in wheel chairs, on crutches and stretchers carried by soldiers with Red Crosses on their arms. Walking on prosthetic legs, guided by a dog, George Williams led demonstrators asserting their right to petition Congress. Spectators crowding the sidewalks turned to watch and applaud the parade witnessing our nation's first response to the sacrifice of four hundred eighteen thousand Americans in a war that could not be evaded.

Speaking from the Capitol steps, "Shouting Hell No! We won't go again!" George Williams mourned our nation's losses insisting "they didn't die for the honor and glory of our country; they had their lives taken away from them!"

The veterans returned to their villages and cities vandalizing Draft Offices, burning Draft cards, and breaking into an Air Force base, pouring blood on the "Bombs for Peace" of General Curtis Le May's Strategic Air Command who threatened to drive Communists "back into the Stone Ages."

Singing – "We've had a bellyful of war" – veterans were grateful to be alive, They had defeated Germany and Japan, and returning home anticipated a peaceful future. But that was not to be. They were dismayed listening to strident voices saying: "now we will do to Stalin what we did to Hitler." Voices exacerbating fear of the "Red Menace" now occupying half of Europe. Peace seemed only a brief interval between wars as nations tested more destructive bombs. Gold Star Mothers gathered at the White House fence singing – "I didn't raise my boy to be a soldier to kill some other mother's son." An Air lift enabling Berlin to survive seemed a rehearsal for another war. Feeling betrayed, anguished veterans recognized as insanity the policy of containing our enemies by "mutual assured destruction."

This was a time of scoundrels. A time for thinking the unthinkable, developing more powerful nuclear weapons with "Kill Ratios" predicting twenty million "Acceptable Losses." A time for an expanding warrior culture driven by the military and the defense industries with demagogic Senators pursuing non-existent spies in high places. A raging fever infected a nation betrayed by subversives, identified by informers, with Department of Justice lists jailing thousands of innocent political activists refusing to sign loyalty oaths. On our Northern border, from dawn to dusk, civilian Watchers of the Ground Observer Corps scanned the Northern skies to provide early warning of Russian bombers. Homeowners dug back-yard bomb shelters while school children crawled beneath desks to practice shielding their bodies from atomic radiation. Air Raid Sirens tested every thirty days maintained a pervasive feeling of dread.

Dismissed as clueless idealists attempting to stop the atomic arms race, Veterans led by George Williams continued marching and protesting until June 1950 when North Korea invaded the South, and General MacArthur sent troops to the Chinese border. America was at war again and George Williams despaired, thinking peace an impossible dream.

George Williams, writing about what he had witnessed asked: "Will there ever be an end to wars? Will the killing fields forever be sowed with the seed of each generation doomed to kill or be killed? Is Cain and Abel the only narrative possible in the long march of history? If God was ever prosecuted by his victims, would he be convicted of sadistic cruelty? If there is no God, then chaos and extinction are inevitable and we must accept judgment we are unworthy of salvation. The savage pity of war cannot be denied!

Maybe God does not roll dice with the Universe? Perhaps he has a plan? An intelligent order we are unable to see? Good questions."

At a magnificent Madison avenue mansion affectionately called "The Powerhouse", Mayors, Union Leaders, Bankers and Shipping executives lobbied for the Cardinal's support. As an honest intermediary, he helped resolve many of New York's financial and political conflicts; his influence always welcomed. As a man of power, the Cardinal had numerous detractors; rivals jealous of his rise to high office. One opponent said: "That's what happens when you teach a book keeper to read." Some Journalists called him "Cardinal Money bags" as they watched him finance and build more schools and churches. He often visited our troops and blessed their weapons in conflicts derided as "Spelly's Wars".

The Cardinal considered Unions a threat to civic peace. He denounced as Communists, Grave diggers in Catholic cemeteries striking for higher wages. The Cardinal believed dock workers, misled by "Red" agitators, threatened the prosperity of New York harbor. He supported a Crime Commission investigation chaired by his good friend Big Bill McCormack, the Penn Stevedoring Company President who declared: "The labor situation on the New York waterfront generally satisfactory."

"Where is Tommy Gleason?" Father Corridan asked when thinking about the unsolved mystery of his disappearance. Placing his beer glass on the bar he turned to Ed Cronin explaining: "Tommy was one of my best Organizers making reform possible. He attempted to charter an honest local ending dues payments to corrupt officials who allowed the Mob to control the docks. Now, no one knows where he is."

"How long has he been missing?

"Over a year. Some say he's in the river. Some think he's working on the West Coast where they have Hiring halls and no Shape Up."

"So nothing's really changed since my father worked the docks?"

"Nothing except the Dock Wallopers are all ex-cons breaking heads or knee caps with baseball bats monitoring elections so everybody votes right."

"And what about your safety Father?"

"I've been threatened. There's talk of fire-bombing my school. And the Powerhouse is unhappy with what I teach. The Cardinal says Unions are un-American and I expect someday I'll be sent upstate far from the docks. That's why I've been educating men like you to continue my work organizing the waterfront. My students are my Apostles recruiting new union members, encouraging them to vote criminals out of office, ending the Shape Up. I also have a Judas! A Police informer who comes to our Happy Hour every Friday when our Soup Kitchen serves hot food to anyone who walks in the door. We are living the oldest story in the Gospels, showing men the light so they will walk with truth and justice and find God's greatest gift, – love for each other! Only love will end the devouring of body and blood in the dark holds of ships. Man-made Hells without mercy or pity where men re-enact Christ's sacrifice while struggling to survive deprived of God's Grace."

To insure Good Order and Discipline, Civil Law is subordinated to Military Law. "Conduct unbecoming an Officer and a Gentleman", punishable by Dishonorable Discharge, loss of pensions and Veterans benefits aborted the careers of many distinguished officers. Responding to a charge of insubordination, Helen defended herself saying: "The tradition rank has its privileges permits intimidation by superior officers. An injustice weakening morale and jeopardizing the military mission."

Colonel Henry Tyler, the Presiding Officer, a West Point graduate displaying decorations affirming years of honorable service, impassively noted her statement before turning and nodding at the other Judges conducting the Court Martial. A Stenographer diligently recorded the proceedings while newsreel cameras, journalists, photographers and spectators crowded the courtroom.

"We who volunteer or are drafted," Helen continued, "give unquestioning obedience to orders, and often our lives. We voluntarily surrender our personal freedom and are entitled to respect. Abuse of our personal dignity is unacceptable."

Several spectators applauded. Colonel Tyler, demanded silence, pounded a gavel on the table calling for order. Then, pausing a moment as the room became quiet the judge replied in a paternal voice: "War is not a garden party. When at war there are some personal freedoms that must be curtailed. No one should violate or abuse the Chain of Command with impunity. Striking a senior-officer jeopardizes the relationship between officers and lower ranks."

"How we fight our wars is as important as why we fight," Helen replied. "What kind of army are we? Do we represent the best qualities of the nation we are defending? Making some soldiers inferior denies our nation's fundamental values, creating prejudice and hostility. If we truly believe all men and women are created equal, how can we accept a system that divides rather than unifies our army? Lower ranks are not sheep led to slaughter. Women are not second class soldiers without rights men take for granted. Giving privileges to some, while denying them to others,

91

is an insult weakening morale. There are no distinctions of rank in body bags."

Applause, and exploding photographer's flashbulbs celebrated her statement. Colonel Tyler pounded the gavel, demanded silence, threatened to clear the courtroom.

"I am accused of assaulting someone I believe assaulted me," Helen continued. I am asked to apologize to someone I think should apologize to me. I believe mutual respect between all ranks regardless of gender will win the war against ignorance, prejudice, and unrestrained authority. What we are now fighting and dying to defeat."

Not intimidated by the audience's applause, the Presiding Officer again pounded the gavel on the table adjourning the hearing. Escorted from the room, Helen Christian struggled through a crowd of reporters shouting questions, pleading for a statement. Flashbulbs popped. Newsreel cameras rolled as Helen's future would now be determined by The Articles of War and the prejudices of three Military Judges.

After an hour of deliberation, the Court officers, without dissent, found Helen Christian guilty of all charges sentencing her to a Bad Conduct Discharge and one year in a military prison.

The Commanding General, reviewing this judgment, set aside this verdict, ordering Helen to immediately begin psychiatric evaluation determining her fitness to continue to serve as an officer in the United States Army Medical Corps.

Unlike other Federal Prisons, "The Sanctuary" provided hospice care for non-violent seniors, wheel chair invalids, consumptives, dementia and Alzheimer cases, and HIV convicts separated from the general prison population. Cell doors were open with prisoners housed in wards with recreation rooms for reading, gambling, or listening to a radio until "lights out" at nine PM. Voices calling from dreams accompanied the cries and moans of sleepless nights that seemed endless. And when not fully awake, days were endured with resignation believing there was no cure for infirmity.

George Williams, sentenced to three years for destroying Federal property, continued to exploit his notoriety as our best known anti-war activist. Arrested while demonstrating at the door of the Pentagon, George Williams recalled the lyrics of a song popular during the first World War.

"I didn't raise my son to be a soldier
I brought him up to be my pride and joy
Who dares to put a musket on his shoulder
To shoot some other mother's darling boy?
Let nations arbitrate their future troubles
It's time to lay the sword and gun away
There would be no war today
If mothers all would say
I didn't raise my son to be a soldier."

Writing to newspapers, speaking at demonstrations, George Williams encouraged burning draft records, damaging weapons, and advocating resistance to military service. A letter from Admiral Gene La Roque, a retired Destroyer Commander, supported George Williams opposition to an expanding military culture when the Admiral wrote: "War is not a noble adventure. There is no honor in saying he gave his life for his country. We steal the lives of these kids. We take it away from them. They don't die for honor and glory. We kill them."

George Williams, replying said: "Peace is not natural, it has to be created with an act of creation requiring a conscious effort of speech and inspiration. Man will always go to war unless he makes peace. It is truly sublime to put an end to war. Can we ever again speak of God after seeing extermination camps? A wondrous creature is Man planting flowers alongside paths leading to gas ovens and crematoriums. Man who reads the Bible every morning before going to his job as a mass murderer – who raises his children on one side of an electrified barbed wire fence detaining millions of innocent human beings. Who is this Man? – How did he happen? – How did he lose his soul, his humanity, his belief in the sacredness of a human life? The cruel winds of history blowing across the killing fields of war answers this question. Nations implode – destined to self-destruct in endless wars shedding innocent blood, sacrificing generations in world-wide horrors motivated by vengeance and self-righteousness. Survival will not be determined by increasing economic and military power but in the increase of understanding. – for only Man – self-respecting law-abiding Man and not his war machines – or self-serving governments – can prevent nuclear Armageddon."

Tommy Gleason's widow, Agnes, like other dock worker's wives, raised her children on the edge of starvation assisted by food stamps, school lunches, and fund-raising rent parties preventing homelessness. Social security benefits, unemployment and disability insurance were unknown to Stevedore families trapped in a cruel peonage similar to what they fled from in Ireland. America's streets were not paved with gold, but work could be had paving them. Enduring the shape-up's inhumanity, living in rat infested tenements, Irish immigrants often yearned for their homeland's rural life. Only the Church's comforting rituals and a Priest's absolution and blessings comforted their Impoverished lives. "Te Absolvo" enabled them to live on nothing more than hope for a better day.

Agnes Gleason's grief turned to anger when Ed Cronin asked about her husband's disappearance. "My Tommy was not one to bow his head and touch a knuckle to his cap to acknowledge the way things are, and the way they will always be," she said. "Father Corridon changed my Tommy, made him ambitious, raised false hopes, educated him far above a poor ignorant dock worker scrambling for work tokens at the shape-ups. It was not in Tommy to be deaf and dumb, so he broke the waterfront's code of silence leaving me a widow with four little ones to raise without a pension."

Her anger subsiding, Agnes Gleason raised a hand brushing back her prematurely grey hair. Her eyes tearing as she continued: "My Tommy was a good provider, he was, not like so many others drinking their pay packets away at the Bars where they could feel sorry for their miserable lives burdened with families they could not support – with every pregnancy not a blessing as the Church says, but a calamity. We were never put out of our flats on to the sidewalks with our children crying and with all our possessions showing our shame and humiliation. It was enough to rip the heart out of a man but not my Tommy who fought for an honest Union. But out in the street, every day, our children see only fools work hard for a living, with shakedowns and running numbers and selling drugs how you get to wear fancy clothes in a world where the Mob and Bosses rule everything. We live and work and die in Hell's Kitchen and that's the truth no matter what the Church says about redemption and salvation. Father Corridan is a good man, and he means well, but I can never forgive him for what he did to my Tommy and all the other workers with strikes and all the children going hungry and some men with cracked heads and broken legs and not ever able to do a hard day's work again. And every night, alone in my bed of grief, I reach out to touch someone who is not there, my Tommy, who was such a good and loving man, who will never again be there to comfort me in the here and now, and not in the hereafter."

Only after years patrolling in rain or snow or hot summer heat, pounding sidewalks for eight hours a day can a policeman expect to have a desk job in an air conditioned Precinct Station. No longer a "Rookie" cop, smart in the ways of the street, Rick Riley hesitated before reluctantly replying to Ed Cronin's questions, for breaking the code of silence can lead to embarrassing headlines and reprimands. Rick Riley believed what he knew about waterfront crime had best be kept to himself because no one loved a "snitch" and loose lips can kill.

There were some peaceful days without much doing until another ship arrived and Stevedore work gangs frantically unloaded and then loaded freight, shortening "turn-around time", benefiting themselves and ship owners. Now finding an hour to meet Ed Cronin in a neighborhood bar, after a few beers and boiler-makers, Rick Riley explained what patrolling "Hell's Kitchen" was really like.

"We're called 'New York's Finest,' when to tell the truth, we're cops who ignore shakedowns, looking the other way while patrolling Hell's Kitchen's 'no man's land' where everyone has their hand out protecting the numbers game, loan-sharking, prostitution and drugs, making an honest man ask – where does all the money go? Ruthless Dock Wallopers make sure worker's vote right in fixed elections paying their dues to the gangsters running the Unions and no investigating Commission will change what keeps the powers that be fat and happy. The Governor, the Mayor and the District Attorney know which side their bread is buttered on when there is an election, and so I do my job the best I can, counting the years until I draw my pension.

It's shameful, pitiful, evicting families and all their possessions out onto the sidewalks when they can't pay the rent. It's a hard, dirty job for someone who was once an Altar Boy reciting his daily catechism teaching love and forgiveness. Where the hell is God? I ask. How can he let these poor kids starve? At night, when I take off my badge and uniform, I stand in the shower trying to feel clean again knowing what sin is truly like. Something you do to your soul that can't be washed away with soap and water.

I'm not any kind of Saint. I've had more than my share of free meals at the local Diner, and traffic ticket Pay-offs from Truckers who'd lose a day's pay going to court. I try to keep juveniles from going bad, and never bother panhandlers and the homeless unless they block traffic or are a danger to themselves or anybody. I'm a good cop, proud of my uniform and what I do for a living. You might say - I'm a straight arrow in a bent society."

Joe Ryan, President of ILA Local 824, known as "The Pistol Local", believed in being a "Good Samaritan" – for everyone deserves a second chance in life. Testifying to the New York Waterfront Commission, he explained how his belief in charity compelled him to give membership cards to 200 paroled convicts despite the fact thirty percent were guilty of manslaughter, murder, rape, and other felonies. After joining the Union they became ruthless 'Dock Wallopers", thugs demanding payoffs from shape-ups, shakedowns, and other criminal activities benefiting Joe Ryan and the politicians protecting him. Joe Ryan's "Hell's Kitchen" childhood taught him all he needed to know about the brutality required to grasp and hold office in a tough dock workers Union. Of medium height, his flaming red hair and aggressive behavior made him look like the middleweight boxer he once hoped to be. His friendships with Mayors and "Big Bill" MaCormack, a Stevedoring Company executive, and Commission Chairman, insured that waterfront crime would flourish even after several intensive city and state investigations.

Joe Ryan did not fear Father John Corridan's attempt to bring the rule of Law to the docks. Many "Bleeding-heart do-gooders", social workers and gospel-singing Salvation Army soldiers tried to reform the waterfront and failed. Tough-talking, hard drinking Father Corridan, with sermons of Christ, Calvary, and sacrifice had little impact on hard-working union members. With help from his "Dock Wallopers", and some bribery, Joe Ryan won every election.

On the wall of Joe Ryan's office a large American flag was accompanied by signed and framed photographs of previous ILA Union Leaders, politicians, Cardinals, Bishops and major league baseball players affirming his reputation as New York's Waterfront Boss. Joe Ryan's office door was always open to anyone asking for help. Every evening, after work, seated behind a large mahogany desk, Joe Ryan leaned back in his chair and with a nod or a smile or wave of his hand granted or withheld favors to loyal dues paying members. Feeling the sublime joy generosity bestows on a man with power, Joe Ryan felt confident his presidency of the union would be forever.

Encouraged by Father Corridan, promising to replace shape-ups with a Hiring hall, Mike Bowers ran as a Union President pledged to fight waterfront crime and negotiate better contracts with Stevedore companies. When Ed Cronin, monitoring the election campaign for the Xavier Labor school asked to see Joe Ryan, he reluctantly agreed, confident he could defend his record serving the dock workers' best interests.

Raising a hand, pointing a large Havana cigar at Ed Cronin, Joe Ryan challenged the fairness of this Inquiry into his leadership.

"I made Mike Bowers what he is today," Joe Ryan replied. "He came from nowhere, a nobody with nothing but muscles and no brain. And then Corridan gives him big ideas, and Bowers turns against me, running for a better union."

Pausing to draw on a cigar, Joe Ryan shook his head, adding in a mournful voice. "He's got no loyalty. No friendship. This Union was once a joke, got no respect from anybody until I took over. Now the Mayor, the Governor, the ship and dock owners listen when I speak."

A ringing phone interrupted his reply. He picked it up and shouted "No calls!" before slamming down the receiver. "There's always been more men then jobs on the docks," Joe Ryan continued. "And when there's no ships, there's no work for anyone no matter what Father Corridan tells dock workers. Shape ups puts men to work where and when they're needed, which is why the Waterfront Commission approved shape ups necessary to the prosperity of New York Harbor."

Ed Cronin turned a page of his notebook and set down his pen before replying: "What Xavier's against is the violence, the brutality, the extortion Stevedores must endure to feed their families. They worry what happened to Tommy Gleason could happen to them."

Joe Ryan put down his cigar, leaned forward in his chair, shaking his head, shouting: "How the hell should I be responsible for what's happened to Tommy Gleason? He's not the only guy run off and just disappear. Maybe got tired of his wife? Got another woman? Maybe fell down, hit his head and got amnesia? You should ask Mike Bowers about Tommy and all them posters, making Tommy into something he's not. Bowers thinks he knows everything there is to know about unions and the waterfront since he went to your damn labor school."

The Patriot

FOUR

Doctor Marvin Franken, MD, leaned back in his chair, raised both hands, pressed his palms together and in an unsympathetic voice said to Helen: "Determining your fitness before reassignment to active duty requires a new understanding of your job. Becoming emotionally involved with a patient is unprofessional."

Seated across the desk from the Psychiatrist, Helen hesitated before replying: "I don't believe there are regulations against falling in love."

Nodding agreement, Dr. Franken replied in a commanding voice: "Common sense should govern your behavior. Favoring one patient over others who also need your personal attention is unacceptable."

Again hesitating, and after a long pause, Helen asked: "How can I not feel what I feel? How can I fail to respond when a patient shows me what it is to love and be loved in return? I'm only human; and when caring for the dead and dying I find myself returning to life – re-entering the world after enduring a great personal sorrow – how can I ignore the promise of a new love? – how can I not follow my heart, for the heart always knows where I truly live in the deepest and fullest sense of that glorious word – home. Before I met George Williams I was homeless and certainly home is where the heart is."

Dr. Frankin turned in his chair, looked down at a dossier on his desk and read for a moment before replying: "You have an excellent record Helen, many commendations, it would be most unfortunate to not return you to active duty."

Helen sat upright in her chair staring at Dr. Frankin, thinking of a reply. Then, after a long pause, said: "I believe in my future with George Williams which will happen by my believing in it. What some might call – a belief in God."

"Ah yes! God!" Dr. Frankin answered. "He's the one who protects drunks, fools, and the United States of America!"

Helen refused to laugh at Dr. Frankin's reply. "Perhaps George Williams is a gift from God?" Helen said. "Perhaps it is possible for something lasting – something beautiful – to emerge from the horrors of this war – perhaps that something is – love? I am no longer afraid of loving again, Dr. Frankin. I no longer fear being hurt like when my fiance was reported dead and I became convinced anyone I loved would die and leave me in pain. I said – never again to love. – No more love! And then I met George Williams and discovered what it would be for two becoming one – growing old together – discovering ourselves in each other – achieving a deep communion – the ecstasy of being more fully alive – reborn in a union that requires no words."

Dear Helen,

George Williams dictated into a tape recorder: "Living behind bars with a bed, sink, and toilet as my home for the next three years – inflicts little hardship. Eating, sleeping and exercising in the prison yard provides time to understand my life as I do not want to disappear without learning who I am and what I can achieve. I prefer not to die – knowing nothing – loving nothing – accepting pain as a condition of my existence; believing doubt and darkness the cost of experiencing every consequence of living and dying. I am a prisoner for refusing to accept lies that determine our nation's moral character for in a free society some are guilty, all are responsible, and with silence giving consent, our government's unlimited power corrupts our nation's soul.

My life has been an adventure in which my spirit made a bargain with God knowing that love is the bridge between the living and the dead enabling us to feel empathy. Perhaps my life's purpose is to discover in the business of living, the reason for living, finding the way to myself – for there is no achievement without a vision – no consummation without faith as we experience the mystery that happens whenever we are true to ourselves as fragile human beings serving truth, justice and freedom."

Truth – Justice – Freedom – without these concepts – these basic values – a nation must surely perish for lies, injustice and servitude are toxic, poisoning the moral energy that makes a responsible human society possible.

And where does a nation's moral energy come from? Who possesses the power of salvation? How can Truth – Justice – and the Freedoms of our past be resurrected?

Who will lead us out of today's wilderness of mendacity, ignorance and hatred?

Good questions.

Love,
George

Walking past crowded waterfront docks revived Ed Cronin's memory of his father unloading ships from London, Bremen, Naples, Bombay, and Hong Kong. Cities he hoped to someday see. Working with hand hooks and cargo nets, four thousand Stevedores manually serviced freighters docking at one of the harbor's 750 piers. Exhausting labor – with torn ligaments, fatal accidents and premature heart attacks crippling their lives. In neighborhood Soup Kitchens and crowded waterfront bars, burned-out, broken, unemployed men, old before forty, drank their lives away as they tried to recall vanished strength.

In 1945, at the end of WWII, new workers arrived from Europe to replace the dead and dying. Impoverished immigrants; human flesh and blood feeding a corrupt peonage system operated by the criminal International Longshoreman's Association paying protection to the Gambino and Anastasia Mafia families.

As a boy Ed Cronin enjoyed watching the arrival of giant luxury liners debarking smiling Celebrities – Mayors, Governors, and Movie Stars – posing for Newsreel cameras before driving off in limousines escorted by wailing motorcycle sirens confirming their importance and power.

New York's magnificent harbor, the "Gateway to America", was also a sewer flushing out to sea the industrial waste of a hundred upriver factories, cities and villages.

Ed Cronin recalled seeing bloated, chalk-white corpses of men who were not deaf and dumb when alive, floating belly-up past docks where breathing putrid flesh, manure and rotting fish odors were a normal childhood experience in "Hell's Kitchen."

Protected by "Dock Wallopers", demagogic speeches by corrupt Union Bosses ruled the docks where the Shape-up, kickbacks and violence seemed forever immutable.

Visiting waterfront Bars, Ed Cronin described to dock workers the changes provided by new Labor laws guaranteeing rights that will only be established by demanding them. Strikes and picketing were now legal in the fight for more pay, benefits and fair hiring practices. For the first time – ending Shape-ups, kickbacks and loan-sharking were now more than futile hopes.

The days required to unload and load ships – "Turn-around Time" – determined ship owners' profits and "slow-downs" gave

Union Leaders more leverage when negotiating better working conditions.

Ignoring this advantage, Joe Ryan, President of ILA Local 824, the notorious "Pistol Local" served the best interests of the Stevedore Companies, employing violence to remain in office.

Arguing – "Joe Ryan must go" – Ed Cronin evoked little enthusiasm from the men gathered around him at waterfront Bars. Some were hostile.

"Who the hell do you think you are?" one angry Stevedore shouted, his face flushed with drink. "You come here telling us what to do and we get our heads cracked or knees broken listening to preaching from that God-all-mighty Priest who never did a day's work in his life. Leave well enough alone, I say. Vote against Ryan – you end up in the river with no one to take care of your wife and children."

Several workers in the smoke-filled Bar shouted agreement. Some nodded. The Bartender refilled beer mugs as one Stevedore, raising his glass exclaimed: "I'll drink to that! Yes, I will!"

A sad, angry worker responded, shaking his head, shouting: "Poor Tommy Gleason and Father Corridan. They closed down 118 piers for 25 days and all we got for their trouble was another Waterfront Crime Commission saying there's nothing wrong on the docks. If you ask me there ain't no truth and there ain't no justice in this life no matter what you say." In a consoling embrace, his arm around Ed Cronin's shoulder, he advised: "if you want to stay alive maybe you should peddle your dead fish somewhere else. Believe me – bucking Joe Ryan ain't good for your health!"

When Ed Cronin walked to the end of a pier and looked down at the water and thought about where the Hudson began, he imagined winter snow and rain falling on Adirondack mountain peaks, melting flakes and rain drops forming rivulets that became streams and creeks tumbling over rocks forming whitewater rapids creating a mighty river.

Ever flowing out to sea, past a hundred rural towns and villages, the turbulent Hudson carried off to eternity memories of the brutal lives of hard-working immigrants mourned only by sea gulls.

For more than a century, this magnificent harbor became the living Hell of intimidated men, threatened by violence, compelled to pay Union dues to criminals.

And at night – walking the waterfront – thinking about the exploited men working on the docks, Ed Cronin listened to the murmuring stream lapping against ship's hulls, quietly beautiful – with sleeping Tugboats moored at the piers, waiting for dawn, while Ferries endlessly crossed the river.

After work – to clear his brain – and wipe out the day's fatigue, – Ed Cronin walked along the docks past crowded Piers where trucks and railroad freight cars waited to load and deliver cargo to the cities, towns and villages of America. He thought about four thousand Stevedores who every day lifted one hundred thousand tons of freight using the same rough hands and bent backs of slaves who built the Pyramids and constructed the Roman roads.

As a Prisoner of War, Ed Cronin recalled looking up at the stars – the same Constellations rotating over "Hell's Kitchen" evoking thoughts about his life. After he is dead and buried and forgotten what will mark his passage through Time?

Perhaps – the meaning of his existence will be his Labor organizing work on the waterfront?

Like Father Corridan, Ed Cronin now had a vocation. A mission he must accomplish for his life to have value.

Walking past the Warehouses and Bars along West street, his feelings intensified by memory, Ed Cronin determined to always truthfully say what he sees – for once we begin to see we are challenged to see more – not less. Surely the world doesn't change the balance between good and bad. Evil will always remain as Man struggles to survive in an ocean of anguish evoking despair. Certainly there are people in this world dedicated to Evil – but without their example – how should we recognize good?

Walking along West street, recruiting votes for reforming a Union, Ed Cronin's appeals were often interrupted by Joe Ryan's "Goons" opposing Father Corridan's hope that ballots and not bullets will bring peace and justice to the waterfront. When a crowded Bar exploded in anger ejecting hecklers, Ed Cronin left the room to walk the now silent piers, with dark shadows cast by streetlights erasing evidence of the violence ignited by hatred, alcohol, and Union politics. A peaceful waterfront was no impossible dream and Ed Cronin believed he could make that hope come true. Crossing West street away from the river, Ed Cronin heard footsteps following him. He stepped into a darkened doorway to listen, hearing only an alley cat rummaging a garbage can as somewhere in "Hell's Kitchen" Police sirens wailed, guarding the nights where crime had become an ubiquitous blood-stained fact of city life. Ed Cronin continued walking, the footsteps behind him following his long-legged strides. He stopped, turned, looking back into the shadows and saw nothing to fear, thinking himself misled by his wartime acute sense of danger.

Then, suddenly, someone rushed out of the darkness and clubbed him behind his ear. Staggering – struggling to remain on his feet – fighting to clear his vision – Ed Cronin turned, and swinging wildly with his right arm, hit his assailant hard on jaw – becoming a brutal street fighter pounding his attacker's ribs, blackening his eyes; hitting – left – right left – right – left –right – a savage response to a surprising attack. Ed Cronin felt invincible. He could still defend himself, anytime, anywhere. No matter the odds. Then, with an angry cry – a baseball bat struck the back of Ed Cronin's head – striking again – breaking both knees – dropping him to the sidewalk like a sack of dirt, a trail of blood flowing from his ear.

A mournful, prolonged cry of a Tug boat horn signaled the departure of another ship sailing to a foreign shore with silence the only commentary from the waterfront's deaf and dumb.

Finding Ed Cronin unconscious in a sidewalk "Dumpster", a surprised Sanitation worker rescued him moments before his battered body was fed into the truck's Compacter.

Awakening in St. Vincent's Hospital's Intensive Care Ward, breathing thru a ventilator, needles puncturing his arm delivering plasma, saline solution, and antibiotics, Ed Cronin looked up at Old Tom's worried face and attempted a smile.

"Those Bastards can't kill an Irishman," he said, his voice muffled by an oxygen mask.

"Joe Ryan's gone too far – this could cost him the election," Old Tom replied holding Ed Cronin's hand.

"I wouldn't be too sure. Beat up one, scare the hell out of four thousand making me an example of what can happen when you oppose him."

"Father Corridan's got the police working, spoke to the Mayor and the Governor, he did."

"I got in a couple of good ones," Ed Cronin boasted, attempting a smile. "Broke a few ribs."

"You're your Father's son," Old Tom said, "a fighter he was, to speak the truth."

"The Goons did my knees."

"It will be crutches for you for months."

"What hit me?"

"A bloody baseball bat was in the Dumpster with you."

"Could of been a gun."

"They didn't want you dead. Alive – everyone will remember what happens when you cross Joe Ryan."

Dear Helen,

George Williams wrote from prison – "writing you is a form of prayer. A Communion enabling me to give myself to you – for I take possession of myself when writing. Communicating with you – comes from my ability to communicate with myself, and knowing myself – opens the door to our hearts where we never stop giving or receiving free of the delusions that confuse love with lust. We are no longer blind to the wisdom of the heart where knowledge comes from pain and suffering.

Suffering enables us see into our heart and grasp the truth about what we feel. A hunger for completeness – the most urgent desire of our soul.

The fullness of our lives is in the hazards of life we must overcome – thru love.

What survives is love – where two are united – becoming inseparable.

To love means to lose yourself in the beloved.

Prisoners form friendships that are the highest form of love. A concern for each other's health and comfort while sharing the most intimate details of their lives. For ten, twenty years, for lifetimes behind bars they walk, talk and eat together in daily routines that can only be endured through deep and abiding friendships. Like old married couples they grieve over their loss when illness or time takes their companion. Widowed, in pain, they withdraw from the prison community refusing a new relationship. They become "Loners" serving their sentence in self-imposed solitary confinement.

Without the comfort of their lost love they become 'Stir crazy'. Reluctant to leave their cells, talking to themselves until they die with no one to mourn their passing for love's power is infinite."

Love of Man inspired Father John Corridan's vocation. His childhood in "Hell's Kitchen" burdened him with knowledge of the suffering stoically endured by friends and family. What angered him and motivated his career as the "Waterfront Priest", was his Parishioners acceptance of their poverty of mind and spirit. Hunger, unemployment, disease, alcoholism, criminal exploitation and death at an early age were the only future they could imagine. Fleeing a devastating Famine they brought with them – a Famine of the spirit – despair – the absence of hope that a better life was possible. They would forever remain ignorant dock workers – even though God's in his Heaven and all's not well in "Hell's Kitchen".

Education made change possible. Teaching self-esteem, and awareness of life's possibilities – becomes another kind of Communion. The Xavier School was a Resurrection where transforming the waterfront could become more than a dream.

Defying the Powers maintaining and exploiting corruption, Father John Corridan was at war – and Disciples like Tommy Gleason and Ed Cronin were casualties.

Ed Cronin raised his arm to welcome Father Corridan as he entered his hospital room.

The Priest smiled and grasped his hand, waiting at the bedside before saying a brief prayer.

"I hope that's not Last Rites you're giving me," Ed Cronin murmured, his voice indistinct behind a face mask and breathing tube. "The Doctors say I'm not going anywhere soon."

Father Corridan nodded. "My prayers for you will be answered."

"I'll hold you to that, Father."

"You're front page news," Father Corridan explained. "The city's in a glorious uproar – what's happened to you could happen to anybody who doesn't keep his mouth shut. And more people realize that than ever before."

Ed Cronin raised his head from the pillow. Doubting what he heard.

"All the old criminal relationships are threatened," Father Corridan continued. "And for the first time the Powers that be are afraid. The Powerhouse is worried. They're losing control. The deceptions of the Mayor, Governor, politicians, Stevedore Companies, and Crime Commission are becoming unacceptable. Believe me – you took a hit in a worthy cause."

"I'm glad to hear that."

"The men are beginning to believe an honest Union is possible. They hear what you and Mike Bowers have been telling them. They're coming together in a way they never did before, becoming a brotherhood, restoring their pride and dignity as men. It's an awakening."

A Nurse entered the room. They remained silent as she read the Monitor and recorded vital signs. Smiling a greeting at the Priest, she quietly disappeared like a vanishing white ghost.

"You're needed, more than ever, Edward. You're place is here, on the waterfront."

"Maybe. After six months of Rehab."

"I visit the Bars and see the solidarity that's crying out for the leadership men like you and Mike Bowers can provide."

"It's you they respect, Father. Only you and your school can change their lives."

"I'll not be here forever, Edward. My work must continue long after I'm gone."

"Gone? How can there be an Xavier Labor school without you?"

"Nothing lasts forever. I'm a Parish Priest who must go wherever they send me. And there are some who are unhappy with what I've been doing. Inciting dock workers to strike. Arousing impossible hopes. Disturbing the peace. Neglecting my other duties – threatening the money made exploiting men's ignorance of their rights. And when I'm gone, the school's future will depend on men like you who see what's needed and are working to make it happen."

"Have you been reassigned?" Ed Cronin said, worried.

"No. Not yet," Father Corridan replied. "The political pressure on the Cardinal is more than he can withstand. He has more to consider than Xavier's future."

"How can it survive without you?" Ed Cronin asked, his voice, under the face mask, breaking.

Father Corridan reached out holding Ed Cronin's hand, comforting him. "They will find someone to replace me."

"Where will you go?"

"Upstate New York."

"As far from the waterfront as possible."

"Yes," Father Corridan admitted. "But I'll still be here on the waterfront every time a better contract is negotiated. Whenever dock workers fight for their legal rights. Whenever their humanity is recognized and respected I'll be there. Truth and justice cannot be denied."

Helen's secret strength, – her hands – had become insensitive. She no longer felt the warmth of living flesh when pressing her fingers to a pulse counting heartbeats. Changing bandages, inserting catheters, looking into the haunted eyes of dying boys, hearing their heart-breaking cries – compelled her to emotionally distance herself from the horror – as if what she could not feel – did not happen.

Stress numbed her sense of touch – her body rebelling against the unbearable. Ugly red rashes discolored her hands. Persistent sores and scabs appeared. Embarrassed by what she thought Stigmata – Helen wore white cotton gloves to conceal her shame.

Were the bandages on the wounds she touched – Holy? she wondered. Is she witnessing the inhumanity of man – making war against the goodness, truth and beauty of life? Am I sinning by silence – when I should be protesting?

Relieved of her duties until her hands recuperated, Helen visited Ed Cronin.

Seated in a wheel chair, he saw Helen enter the crowded visitor's Lounge. Waving his arm, he wheeled across the room to meet her at the door. Sitting upright in his chair, he raised his hand in a smart military salute.

"Good to see you Lieutenant."

Helen laughed, shaking her head, not returning the salute. Then, following him into the room said: "Read all about you in the papers. A Waterfront hero."

Turning the wheelchair to face her, Ed Cronin smiled: "No good turn ever goes unpunished."

"So I've been told," Helen replied: "However, I prefer my heroes alive."

"That's me," Ed Cronin said, raising his voice, almost shouting: "Alive and well and when my knees heal, I'll return to the docks."

"And get yourself killed."

"That's possible. Never ran away from a good fight. Always finish what I started."

Helen turned to look out the window into the garden where patients and visitors were walking. With her back to Ed Cronin she said: "Life's so complicated, Peacetime seems only a pause between wars."

"Some are necessary," Ed Cronin replied. "What we are fighting for on the waterfront can't be evaded."

"I wouldn't want to lose you," Helen said, reaching out to hold his hand. "You're still important to me."

"And you to me," Ed Cronin replied. "Can never forget the good times. What we felt for each other then. But what's next? What do we do with our lives?"

"Live," Helen said. "Live."

"But How? How can we go on accepting the unacceptable?"

Helen paused a moment, hesitating, searching for words before replying: "We are imperfect beings in an imperfect world – Life is too precious to be thrown away for something that will never happen. Only in scriptures will you find Paradise."

"I wouldn't be too sure, Helen. Change is possible if we resist – protest – risk our lives in a worthy cause. The streets and docks are another battlefield in a war that will never end."

Dear Helen,

"One World or None" is more than a hopeful slogan. One World, ruled by Law, is the goal we sought fighting WWII's "Moral War" – destroying twenty million lives. Can a war be judged "good" or "moral" when great cities are reduced to rubble and mass graves? Avoiding Fascism's dark age of hatred, fear, and captive minds I discovered how close we came to barbarism when failing to achieve lasting peace. Fighting over national boundaries to preserve our democracies – we sacrificed our humanity as we descended ever-deeper into despair. Hiroshima – Nagasaki – Auschwitz – abolished past limits on our behavior.

"My Country right or wrong," proclaimed Carl Schurz in 1859, describing true patriotism as the belief – "If right – to be kept right – and if wrong – to be set right." – This I believe with all my heart and soul is patriotism.

Describing what I have witnessed, thought, felt and experienced is how I try to understand the world I have returned to. Why I am alive. I have seen the tenderness of a mother nursing her child, the dreams and high expectations brightening the eyes of youth, the dignity and courage of old age. I have been deeply moved by love, inspired by devotion, encouraged by the confidence of others sustaining my persistent hopes. I have been blessed by friends, health and courage, and the confident belief I am not alone in this world but a part of some greater plan that includes my own personal destiny.

As an old Gospel prayer explains: "I once was lost – but now I'm found – was blind – but now I see."

Love,
George

The "Bermuda Triangle", also known as "The Devil's Triangle", is an area in the Atlantic ocean extending from Florida to the Bahamas, then North to Bermuda, returning on a Southwest course to the Florida mainland. Here, for five hundred years, the unexplained loss of ships and sailors created one of the sea's great mysteries. In 1872 the "Ghost Ship" Mary Celeste was sighted under full sail, with no seamen on board. In 1921, the Carrier ship SS Carroll Deering disappeared with no evidence of what happened to the Captain and eleven man crew.

Speculation about the cause of these and other maritime disasters in the "Bermuda Triangle" included underwater earthquakes forming holes in the ocean into which ships disappeared, freak waves capsizing hulls, air bombs produced by methane gas rising from the ocean floor, electronic fogs and other supernatural forces defying rational explanation.

Navigational errors were never adequately investigated by a Court of Inquiry with one exception.

Flight 19's disappearance, recorded in Flight Logs at NAS Fort Lauderdale, disclosed how fourteen aviators and five aircraft vanished. Flight 19's leader, Commander Charles Taylor, during WWII, had been lost three times, ditching his plane in the ocean. Nevertheless, his poor navigational history did not disqualify him for assignment as an Instructor training student pilots.

Without visual landmarks, over ocean navigation required accurate "Dead Reckoning" tracked on a continuously updated chart board recording course made good after allowing for compass deviation. Air speeds, adjusted for head, tail and cross winds, determines ground speeds multiplied by time, computing the distance each course is flown. Looking down at the sea, estimating wind direction and force by wave heights, pilots correct for wind drift affecting their intended course. With only a chronometer, compass, and an accurate chart board, the ancient art of "Dead or Deduced Reckoning" was still a navigator's most essential skill.

On December 5th, 1945, at 2:10 PM, five Torpedo bombers, four flown by student pilots with seven crewmen aboard, led by Commander Charles Taylor, departed NAS Fort Lauderdale on a training flight to a bombing target in the Bahamas.

Like Admiral Thomas Kinkaid's stubborn eight day attack on Kiska, an island abandoned by the Japanese, Commander Charles Taylor did not question his own judgment – checking computations – admitting no possibility of error – feeling his skill and pride as a leader challenged – he disobeyed instructions to pass leadership of flight 19 to a student pilot.

At 3:30 PM Commander Taylor reported his compass malfunctioning.

At 3:45 PM, confused, Commander Taylor said he could not see land and seemed off course.

At 3:50 PM a student pilot was recorded saying: "If only we fly west we would get home."

At 4:45 PM, Commander Taylor, unfamiliar with the Florida Bahamian area, was now disorientated.

At 5:50 PM a Radar bearing located Flight 19 east of Smyrna Beach Florida heading North, out into the vast Atlantic. This position, transmitted to Flight 19 was not acknowledged.

At 7:04 PM Flight 19's final transmission was heard.

At 7:27 Two PBM Mariner sea planes departed to search for Flight 19.

At 7:50 PM one Mariner disappeared from Radar. No wreckage was ever recovered.

Admiral Hyman Rickover, the officer most responsible for the development of Navy Nuclear power once wrote:

"Responsibility is a unique concept. It can only reside and inhere in a single individual. You may delegate it, but it still is with you. You may disclaim it, but you cannot divest yourself of it. If responsibility is rightfully yours, no evasion or ignorance or passing the blame can shift the burden on someone else. Unless you can point your finger at the man who is responsible when something goes wrong, then you never have anyone really responsible."

Who is responsible for casualties?

The President who sends soldiers to war?

The Congress who may or may not vote for war?

Admiral Harry Hill at Tarawa? Admiral Thomas Kinkaid at Kiska?

Commander Charles Taylor leading Flight 19 to disaster?

Our Leaders too often deny the reality they are confronting – truly believing what they believe – failing to question their judgment – reluctant to admit the possibility of error maintaining the appearance of infallibility. Disinformation based on official statements becomes the truth that cannot be denied without giving "aid and comfort" to the enemy. Defeats become Victories. "A bodyguard of lies" protects the truth without which nations and armies must surely be defeated. Casualties become the price of freedom and democracy Patriots pay as their civic duty.

For the sun never sets on our passivity as citizens — In the name of Patriotism – we accept leadership bringing recurrent wars as the normal cost of freedom – surrendering our humanity — allowing the perversion of free and honest thought by political demagogues. We are not actors of our fate – but acted upon by destructive forces beyond our control.

Dear Helen:

The moral damage recurrent wars inflict on our society evokes contempt for the rule of Law – insulting life, liberty, and the dignity of all citizens. Ambitious men — without moral scruples – achieve power when a "silent majority" remains complicit in their behavior. The true Patriot, opposing the destruction of human liberty – fights to preserve all he loves about his country.

"As our case is new," said Abraham Lincoln, "so must we think anew and act anew. The dogmas of the quiet past are inadequate to the stormy present."

Like Henry David Thoreau, I believe in non-cooperation with Evil – and the true place for a just man is often prison. By refusing to be an agent of corruption and injustice – by non-violent civil disobedience – I hope to prevent further abuse of our national conscience.

Patriots fighting and dying for what they believe – are rightly honored in national cemeteries, monuments and history books preserving memory of their sacrifice. But other Patriots, choosing to live for their country thru Civil disobedience — deserve equal honor fighting for truth and justice.

Behind bars – I am not disarmed. For "The pen is mightier than the sword" – and my words will go forward into the future – for words like truth, justice and love are common property – they belong to us all.

At night, I dream of a freedom where all my hopes, and every road, lead me out of the darkness and storms of life to living under a golden sky where I am not alone – for you walk with me.

Love,
George

St. Vincent's Emergency Room functioned like a rear-area battlefield medical station treating casualties of Hell's Kitchen's violence and despair. Routine were suicides, gun-shots, stabbings, fractured skulls, smashed knee caps and life-threatening injuries when a failed winch brake, or broken cable brought sudden death to a dock worker.

Old Tom's Food Cart on the docks served more than pork sausages, hot dogs and black coffee. Old Tom was reputed to know all there was to know about what happened on the waterfront enabling him to provide updated news of Ed Cronin's brutal attack.

Old Tom knew who ruled the waterfront. Knew – when the "Hammer of Fate" dropped on a victim, ordering a "hit" – death was inevitable. Only the deaf and dumb lived to work another day. Union Organizers, gaining worker's confidence, threatened to destroy a corrupt system enriching the few by exploiting the many. Keeping Ed Cronin alive and safe until he could walk became Old Tom's most solemn duty.

A dock worker for twenty years, Old Tom at forty, could no longer raise a strong arm and swing a hook, loading and unloading cargo nets. His body was worn-out lifting crates, and he now felt old, breathless and faint climbing up from a ship's hold, endangering other dock workers who urged him to turn in his badge before he dropped dead, releasing a load, killing someone.

The Waterfront was Old Tom's home since stepping off the boat from Ireland. The Food Cart supported and kept him with other hard-working and drinking Stevedores. He determined to never become another derelict sleeping in doorways, "Flop Houses", or Homeless Shelters; wiping car windows for handouts, eating at Charity Kitchens, his final destination the City Morgue and an unmarked grave at "Potter's Field".

As a recovering crime victim, Ed Cronin's hospital room was guarded by a Policeman in a chair tilted back against a wall, reading a newspaper. No visitors other than the District Attorney, Doctors, Nurses, and Old Tom were allowed to enter. After visiting Ed Cronin one morning, before returning to the waterfront, Old Tom had breakfast at the hospital Coffee Shop crowded with medical staff and family visitors. Looking around the room, Old Tom felt he was witnessing a scene from the movie

"The fight for life," an exciting drama performed by dignified Doctors, Surgeons with their white face masks around their necks, young Interns, and pretty Nurses joyously eating, talking, and laughing momentarily free of their life and death responsibilities. He was convinced Ed Cronin would live. Such dedication, by so many devoted people, could not fail.

Seated alone at the rear of the Coffee Shop, cup in hand, unsmiling, a young male Nurse seemed withdrawn. Wearing blue "scrubs", a mask and stethoscope around his neck, wearing a surgical cap, he appeared anxious to finish eating and do whatever task he was assigned to do.

Old Tom finished his breakfast thinking about Ed Cronin's vulnerability to any intruder the Policeman admitted to his room. Nurses checking IV's, administering drugs and feeding patients routinely entered, their only ID their uniforms. What can happen – can happen, Old Tom thought, recalling incidents where the impossible occurred. Convinced only death could prevent Ed Cronin from testifying, Old Tom looked around the coffee shop. An unfinished breakfast on the young male nurse's table aroused Old Tom's fears.

Saint Vincent's elevators were 19th century antiques. Slow moving, with rumbling sounds frustrating passengers rising to a higher floor. Old Tom waited impatiently, looking down at his watch counting minutes, reluctant to use the stairs to climb to Ed Cronin's fourth floor room. Arriving at the door breathless, Old Tom awakened the Policeman asleep in his chair, the newspaper now on the floor at his feet. Entering the room, they interrupted the young Male Nurse holding a large Hypodermic needle leaning over Ed Cronin, preparing to inject his comatose body. Startled by the intrusion, the Nurse dropped the Hypodermic and fled the room.

Dear George,

Yes – we will someday walk together as man and wife – our love providing the energy – the Life Force enabling us to overcome life's challenges. Love is our strength – now and forever – concrete walls and iron bars do not make a prison when love shatters the barriers separating us.

Yes – saving the world is possible – one patient at a time. Suture one bleeding wound – set one fractured leg or arm – make one heart beat again – and mankind's self-destruction is momentarily delayed when love displaces terror and defeats hatred. A hospital ward becomes a battlefield on which the great drama of our lives plays out and we are actors repeating actions and speaking lines that have been heard before – only the ending is unwritten. Will it be – Salvation? – Or Oblivion?

Once upon a time we lived as full human beings now diminished and humiliated by lies displacing truth. "In time of war," said Winston Churchill, "Truth is so precious it must be protected by a bodyguard of lies." – lying is now so ubiquitous we repeat falsehoods as facts – with Mantras like – "Fighting a War to end War!" – "Bombs for Peace" – and "Boots on the ground".

In my mind forever are bitter memories staining my soul. I have seen rising pillars of smoke and flame – not burning corpses but piles of discarded blood-soaked battlefield stretchers filling the air with the odor of charred wood, canvas and human blood – swept away by the hot desert wind – desecrating the beauty of the star-studded North African sky.

I have seen the haunting eyes of the wounded, without protest, accepting Triage and inevitable death.

Love,
Helen

Dear Helen,

How I hate the word "handicapped" – spoken by souls devoid of empathy – blind to what the human heart contains. Empathy enables me – with sightless eyes – enter other minds understanding what I did not see before the war. I feel – not handicapped – but empowered. Walking on prosthetics – becomes a triumph of the will – making me – for the first time in my life – aware of the miracle of mobility knowing there are many degrees of aliveness.

When fully alive, writing fulfills my need to reveal myself – free of the fear of dying unknown and forgotten. Opening my heart – I would hold it in my hand for all the world to see and admire.

Truth is like the stars that cannot be seen except beyond the darkness of the night. And there is no greater truth than life and love are one – and love is difficult and demanding.

Happiness and heartache are entwined, and without experiencing tragedy – would we ever know joy?

I fear wasting my life more than I fear death. Without thinking and writing – what would I be? Who am I without surprise, astonishment and wonder – my mind trying to catch my creative flights?

And so I choose to live rather than allow my life to wear away by the passage of time, believing I am brought into this world to fulfill some unknown task. Failing this responsibility – my life is without meaning.

And the meaning of life is not something we discover – but a choice we make about the way we live – before we die.

Love,
George

Dear Helen,

"With my knees in plaster casts, I travel inside my mind, walking back into my past, with time to think, trying to understand where I am today – and hopefully – discover my future. Joe Ryan's Goons used me to demonstrate the high price of opposing him – with fear deciding the election. We're confronted with the old question of Good versus Evil – the shape-up or the hiring hall – justice or corruption – determined by the choices Union members make. "Give a man crutches and he won't grow legs", they say. Well, there's no doubt – on crutches – I'm walking further and arriving closer to the truth of my life than ever before. Like when FDR was President his enemies cried – "don't let a cripple – cripple the country" – yet – with steel braces on his legs – he saw more than they did and travelled further providing hope for a better world.

It's good to be alive when things are changing and I am contributing to that change. Being a POW also changed who and what I am enabling me to understand other men who hold on to life and face death with dignity and courage. What is that spark of hope that keeps men alive for another day of misery? Where does that vitality come from? Father Lawler says it is God-given – but not all men believe in God – many surrender to fear – feeling only despair.

Some prisoners stopped eating. They remained in their bunks all day and night, withdrawn from their comrades who do not interfere with their dying and death. Other men joke, laugh and tell stories sustaining confidence and hope of liberation. They describe favorite menus, cooking and eating imaginary meals, nourishing childhood memories. They sing and listen to lectures keeping their minds alive – as their emaciated bodies fight off starvation. They are surviving – as slowly, with time – "Mom's door in '44" becomes – "Home alive in 45".

On Bataan, retreating from one defensive line to another in what "Dugout Doug" called – "successful retrograde movements" – we felt betrayed and abandoned. The Stars and Stripes, – the good old USA had failed us. We were truly "The Battling Bastards of Bataan – No Poppa – No Mama – No Uncle Sam" – and no victorious Fleet ever steamed into Manila Bay to rescue an army betrayed by a vain glorious General. Four years later, this tragedy ended in farce as General Macarthur, corn cob clenched between his teeth, head high, wearing a decorated Field Marshall's hat, saluted newsreel cameras as he stepped off a Landing Craft's ramp into eight feet of water – for one comic moment – sinking out of sight. With the bow now properly beached, wearing a dried and pressed uniform, his landing now successfully filmed proclaiming – "I have returned" – words heard around the free world and now immortalized as history.

I cannot forget the indignity and shame of being a POW – turning in upon myself, losing all sense of time, locked in a dark windowless room, alone and forgotten, trying to hold on to what I remembered of my past, fearing my identity as a human being lost forever. Who am I? was a question I could not answer. Weakened by hunger and thirst, light-headed, losing my faith in mankind, I existed in a dismal state half-way between consciousness and death – a Zombie in the land of the walking dead marching thru Hell in a blood-stained T shirt and filthy shorts.

Hope does not spring eternal from the human breast as some Poet's say. Hope is an expectation that can break the stoutest heart."

Love,
Edward

So tell me pretty lady – are there any more at home like you? –
Helen Christian hummed the tune and sang the lyrics remembering
her father's singing while playing a violin, often changing into a
slow and spiritual *Ave Maria*. Closing her eyes, she recalled
descending into the deep and delicious sleep of her childhood –
and now – as a mature woman – she was aware of the pain
enabling her to see into the human heart. Watching Death take so
many young lives – Helen felt not only a deep and abiding sorrow
– but also a feeling of accomplishment when she reached out to
care for the wounded. She learned the most beautiful things in life
cannot be seen – but must be felt with the heart. A belief that made
the inexorable flow of life possible.

Helen now knew what it is to love and be loved in return. No
small blessing. She will marry George Williams, not out of pity,
but as her fulfillment as a human being. Searching for herself she
successfully answered the question – Who am I?

She recognized she was possessed by the infinite power of
love. Not only for patients – but for the world outside her hospital
window. She saw the beauty of a sunrise and sunset, billowy
clouds scudding across the sky, trees and flowers budding in
spring, the wind pressing against her as she walked in a rainstorm
feeling ecstatic at the wonder of her survival. For Helen – Life and
Death were partners – and being alive to love was Life's greatest
gift.

She also wondered: What is happiness?

Indeed – life can be beautiful – and happiness is an awareness
of that beauty. A consciousness that became a powerful current
driving her life to its destiny.

She learned about courage watching Helen Keller's visit the
Rehab Ward. Deaf, dumb and blind at an early age, Helen Keller
showed Helen the joy of a purposeful life. Her hospital visits,
lectures and books inspired the recovery of many disabled
veterans demonstrating no one was crippled If their minds were
free of despair – for everyone could be their own "miracle worker"
and have useful lives. Learning Braille, Helen Keller learned to
speak and write twelve books driven by her determination to live a
full, productive and creative life demonstrating that no matter how
damaged the body – optimism and hope remained powers
everyone possessed.

In the endless waking hours of the night, unable to sleep, Helen imagined herself again swimming in the ocean, fighting for her life as her torpedoed troopship capsized and sank. Scenes of her childhood appeared; her mother drying her body in a soft warm towel as she climbed from a bathtub, brushing her hair, putting on her favorite dress saying – "how pretty you are Helen – how pretty you are."

And then she recalled growing colder in the frigid Atlantic, shivering, her life force ebbing, her arms losing the strength to hold her head above water. Dear God save me, she shouted, save me as a hand reached down and pulled her from the water into a lifeboat. God's hand working the miracle of rescue as she heard gunshots and saw her rescuer fall from a self-inflicted wound, his head blown away. A recurring re-play of rescue and death forever re-appearing in her haunting dreams.

And she often thought about dear Scotty dressed in her white nurses' uniform and cap, her lovely hands folded across her chest, her eyes closed in peaceful sleep as she was lowered into a shallow grave in a green US Army body bag as a Bugler mournfully blew *Taps*.

In Helen's mind – she again heard Scotty saying – love will survive – despite anguish – for the fullness of life is in overcoming the hazards of life – death – and love.

In June 1950, four years after victory in World War II, America went to war again fighting a "Police Action" in Korea". Reservists, interrupting their marriages and careers, were recalled. Selective Service offices – Draft Boards – resumed a human Lottery determining the life or possible death of patriotic citizens who, when compelled to serve, obeyed. Some sought deferments or became Draft Dodgers. "Political Activists" chanting – NO MORE WAR! – END THE DRAFT! – burned their registration cards at the White House fence and vandalized military bases. Dissenters were declared disloyal, unpatriotic, communist dupes, subjected to interrogation by hostile Congressional committees attempting to revive American patriotism.

In "Letters From A Federal Prison" George Williams became leader of the Peace Movement – a voice for reason, justice and the rule of International Law advocating – "One World or None".

Ignoring "Free George Williams" Petitions to commute his sentence, the Federal government attempted to silence this eloquent anti-war activist by denying his mailing, telephone and visitation privileges – holding him incommunicado – apart from the general prison population. Moved to Solitary Confinement, his only exercise pacing back and forth in a small, windowless cell, struggling to maintain his sanity, George Williams ate his meals alone with no one to talk to but hostile prison guards who woke him every two hours for "bed checks". Deprived of sleep, disoriented, after several months of isolation, losing all sense of time, his stirring voice for peace became incoherent, his situational awareness regressed to the consciousness of a dysfunctional child.

A raging fever of patriotism swept across the land confronting the "Red Menace". Traitors were discovered in high office, journalists questioning official statements were fired, mass arrests and hatred of foreigners believed to be spies drove the political careers of scoundrels who aroused such fear of the future that schoolchildren practiced "Duck and Cover" under their desks to survive an inevitable nuclear attack.

"Blacklists" in the Movie and TV industry, and "Red Channels" magazine named subversives, destroying the lives and careers of innocent victims in a savage war on dissent resembling Salem Witch Trials. Public hysteria allowed the government to relocate one hundred twenty thousand citizens of Japanese ancestry to Internment Camps in the barren deserts of the American West. Attempting to maintain Law and Order, ignoring citizens' rights, Police and Guardsmen – firing tear gas and live ammunition – became law-breakers – "Preventative Detention" round-ups ignored the fact non-violent demonstrators' behavior was legal.

In a national moral breakdown, the only response to industrial Strikers fighting for their rights under existing labor laws – was to call-out the National Guard. Tear gas and bayonets restored "Law and Order" while casualties "got what they deserved" – with the Constitution an inconvenient document. Presidents and State Governors published "Enemy Lists" – "Citizen Councils", respectable community leaders – exposed anyone suspected of being Un-American.

Fear and hate replaced – "love thy neighbor" – when Community Activists attempted to overcome housing restrictions on people of color or foreign birth. The great "American Dream" was not for everyone. We became two different nations – "The haves" – and – "The have-nots" – at war with each other. Brutality became an expression of American paranoia when the Police, like an invading army fired live ammunition at peaceful demonstrators.

Hatred and fear – metastasized like cancer – "The Land of The Free and The Home of The Brave" – became a "Police State".

Refusing food, protesting with a prolonged Hunger Strike, George Williams was force-fed with a tube inserted into his nose. After shouting – "America Devours its Young" – George Williams' lips were closed with tape and diagnosed insane, he was moved to the Prison Hospital where, with electrodes attached to his brain, he received a series of therapeutic Electro-convulsive shocks designed to restore his sanity. In a desperate effort to break George Williams' spirit – the heat was turned off in his cell and his prosthetics legs removed. Denied a wheel chair, using his residual limbs and arms, he crawled from his bed to the toilet.

P.T. Barnum, the famous Showman once observed – "There's a Sucker born every minute" – and for a hundred years, his travelling Circus and Museum entertained millions of Americans believing and enjoying whatever he presented.

President Abraham Lincoln also observed – "You can fool some of the people some of the time".

Demonstrating the wisdom of these comments, Dr. Walter J. Freeman, MD, an infamous travelling medical Showman called the "Ice Pick Surgeon", performed several thousand Lobotomies as a miraculous cure for mental illnesses. Calling his therapy – "Psycho Surgery" – he destroyed the frontal lobes of the brain by hammering into them an ice pick inserted through an eye-socket. He toured a nation attracting desperate believers seeking to cure their manic-depression and suicidal thoughts. In twelve days in one State, Barnstorming through West Virginia, Dr. Freeman lobotomized 225 patients reducing them to lives of total disability

– if they were fortunate enough to escape dying from a brain hemorrhage.

Ignoring these tragic results, many American Prison Officials used Lobotomies as an effective way of controlling violent, mentally disturbed inmates by destroying their sensory functions as human beings. Unable to think clearly, talk coherently, unaware of their surroundings, Lobotomized prisoners were ideal inmates – never a disciplinary problem.

In 1305, when England's King Edward reigned, the first writ of "Habeas Corpus" ordered his Officers to "produce the body" held in confinement. Blackstone, the great Jurist called the Writ – "The greatest and most effective petition in all matters of illegal detention. A true safeguard of Liberty." Prisoners held incommunicado relied upon friends and family to free them in a legal process only suspended in the United States during the American Civil War.

Inspired by Clarence Darrow who once freed eight unjustly convicted negroes, Howard Duncan, an activist lawyer, was outraged by George Williams' treatment as a prisoner. As an "Amicus Curie" – "friend of the Court", he filed a Habeas Corpus Writ requiring the government to "produce the body" of George Williams.

"Every Convict, no matter how heinous his crime," Howard Duncan argued, "is entitled to his human dignity. Holding a Prisoner incommunicado, a caged animal in solitary confinement, destroys his ability to connect with the reality that makes him a thinking, feeling, living human being. Solitary Confinement makes rehabilitation and a Convict's return to the general prison population, or civil society, difficult, often impossible."

Many assenting voices responded to Duncan's plea. The presiding Judge, Andrew Jackson Boon, a dignified Presidential appointee from Tennessee, pounding a gavel on the bench, called for order. Replying to Duncan with a polite nod, he paused a moment before saying: "This Court does not dispute your statement – but the facts in this case show a crime has been committed, the Perpetrator indicted, tried, and convicted must serve his sentence subject to Parole. To excuse his past behavior arguing his human dignity is now being abused – violates the fundamental spirit of our Constitution."

Interrupting vigorous applause from spectators, the Judge pounded the gavel. The newsreel cameras turned to Howard Duncan as he removed his eye glasses and held them in his hand a thoughtful moment. Reaching down to the Lectern to pick up a book, raising the spectacles to his eyes, he opened to an underlined page and quoted in a quiet forceful voice: "The spirit and life of the law has not been logic" – Supreme Court Justice Oliver Wendell Holmes argued in a precedent-setting case – "The spirit and life of the Law has been – experience – the felt necessities of the time – the prevalent political theories and intuitions of public policy include the prejudices judges share with their fellow- men. The Law embodies the story of a nation's development through many centuries and cannot be dealt with as if it contained only the axioms of a book of mathematics. In order to know what the Law is – we must know what it has been, and what it tends to become."

The now silent spectators nodded as they thought about the quotation. Judge Andrew Jackson Boon, speaking with a distinct southern drawl, responded: "The felt necessities of the time, Oliver Wendell Holmes referred to, also includes our need to maintain law and order under all circumstances of war and civil unrest. The best interests of society as a whole – becomes the Law of the Land. To believe otherwise – is to welcome chaos. National Security – the greatest good for the greatest number – is the government's greatest responsibility."

A church bell near the courtroom tolled an unexpected accompaniment to his statement. The Judge looked down at his watch to confirm the hour. He nodded at Duncan.

"The felt necessities of the time," Duncan continued, "does not repeal the truth – murder is also murder when perpetrated by our government. Aggressive hostility to dissenters – violence used to secure Law and Order arises from a moral breakdown of the Law – an incapacity to reconcile with each other sharing a common moral vision of our nation. We become fearful citizens hoping for salvation by demagogues in a morally bankrupt society where destroying the dissenting spirit of a minority, by a powerful majority, is accepted as normal. The courage of anyone feeling obligated to resist the destructive forces of fear and hatred – is not revered by the majority of citizens – but despised. I am here today to speak for someone whose voice has been silenced for crying out for truth and justice. George Williams, experiencing and despising war – advocates peace now – saying no more war – Peace is not an impossible dream – but a hope for our future survival as human beings living in a dangerous world. The choice is – truly – "One World or None."

Howard Duncan concluded by saying – "As Supreme Court Justice Robert H. Jackson argued – 'It is not the function of government to keep the citizen from falling into error – it is the function of the citizen to keep the government from falling into error.' A responsibility – a moral challenge – George Williams courageously accepted."

Dear George,

    Howard Duncan's "Friend of the Court", Amicus Curie Brief has generated a firestorm of Petitions asking the President to commute your sentence. – I've been told you will soon be free – free to resume your fight for One World or None! – But what about our world – our future life together? – Will there be nothing but Politics as you continue your fight for Peace Now?

    I must confess wherever I am – I feel you there – see you there – but always present is that painful feeling of missing you – terribly much. Absence does indeed make the heart grow fonder – and I constantly find myself wishing you were here with me and not in prison.

    Love,
    Helen

Dear George,

I have a sudden strong desire to share my thoughts with you. I know not how you will react, but I am hopefully anticipating your understanding of what I mean when I speak about – rapport. That magical state two people achieve with time. Why is it lacking in our relationship? I feel, after all we have been through together we don't seem to be going anywhere. Sometimes it seems we hardly know each other at all.

You seem to give very little of yourself – the basis for any kind of mental spiritual closeness.

There is no correlation between our physical intimacy and our psychological rapport. I have a feeling of something being wrong – because we don't have enough of the meeting of our minds to warrant such strong sexual emotions. For I believe only when two people are mentally and spiritually close, can they, and should they make love. I want ours to have more meaning. I dislike your making meaningless love to me. So that is why I ask – talk to me – talk to me honestly – for I wonder what are we?

Lovers? – Or Friends? – establishing no kind of bond. – George, this is me – Helen – asking you to talk to me. – To give our relationship a chance to develop into an understanding that has integrity and a future.

Love,
Helen

Dear Helen,

In any relationship there is one who gives – and one who receives or "takes". You have been the "giver" in our years together, overwhelming me with the generosity of your love, devotion and care. I know I have failed to adequately respond to your love – my spirit – my head too often is up in the clouds with my thoughts, ambitions and dreams. I am physically there – but not really there for you – failing to meet what you wanted and needed from me. My writing – my fight for peace – my obsession – are all directed at creating a world that does not devour generations of our young.

Perhaps it is too much to ask your forgiveness and acceptance of who and what I am now, and will be in the future. I cannot promise to change who I am and will be in whatever life we will have together.

Can you bear the sorrow, disappointment and frustration of living with someone who is divided in mind and spirit? A man incapable of achieving the "rapport" you have a right to expect from a husband?

We must answer these painful questions. We cannot ignore the simple truth that the golden threads of love do not always succeed in binding lovers together – forever.

Love,
George

At the Xavier Labor school, Ed Cronin discovered his true vocation was to teach and fight another war – an enduring battle against ignorance and poverty. For sixty years, desperate immigrant workers arrived on transatlantic Steamships for a cruel future in a country where unemployment and hunger crushed their spirit – with nothing to look forward to but alcoholism and early death for men, and widowhood for wives.

"Been down so long they can't imagine anything better," Father Corridan commented. "As tenant farmers for heartless Landlords they learned subservience and acceptance of poverty. They knew nothing but how to use a hoe, a rake and a spade. Literacy – reading and writing – was neglected – ignorance and shame destroyed their pride and self-respect. Taunted by cries of 'Greenhorn – Pop Corn – five cents a box' – uneducated immigrants had difficulty assimilating into the great American Dream."

Old Tom confirmed this: – "You can't imagine what it is like not to read and write – separated from what everybody knows – ashamed you're illiterate – hiding you're only a poor ignorant 'Mick'".

"It's insulting to be called dumb," Father Corridan continued. "Knowing little more than your Catechism and a Hail Mary. Illiteracy is a trap few escape in a world of new ideas and opportunities. There's no need to learn your ABC's or put words together to be able to swing a hook or load a cargo net when you're only taught to kneel and pray and be grateful for a day's pay. And for too many years the Church failed to meet its responsibility to educate all the young – not just a select few – sending to America only poor, desperate, cast-offs enslaved by ignorance. A shame that will be with us – I hope not – forever."

Ed Cronin fought a losing battle. After working all day – his students struggled to stay awake. Weary, hopeless, overwhelmed by self-doubt – they dropped out — unable to join 26 letters into words, and words into stories. They were – depressed – despairing – and Ed Cronin shared their hopelessness. Perhaps singing would raise their spirits and help overcome their illiteracy he suggested.

Father Corridan laughed. "A Dock Workers Chorus would be a great achievement. Certainly our Cardinal would be pleased. My God! – Singers for Christ. Choir Boys holding cargo hooks in their hands."

"No," Ed Cronin insisted, "Not Choir boys but hard-working – decent ignorant men struggling to learn their ABC's - one letter, one word at a time.

Ed Cronin recalled marching from a POW camp to the Japanese coal mine following British and Australian prisoners parading with heads high, backs straight, arms swinging forward singing – "It's a long way to Tipperary." Slave Laborers, housed in sordid camps, suffering from hunger, dysentery and dengue fever, they remained His Majesty's proud warriors maintaining rigid military discipline. He believed their high survival rate was due to healing their wounded spirits by singing.

"Sing along with me," Ed Cronin encouraged his students. "Sing along with me. You don't need to be a falling down bar room drunk before opening your mouths and singing. There's more to life then drowning your sorrows in boiler-makers."

Soon the empty seats filled. Enthusiastic dock workers asked to learn songs. "Sing," Ed Cronin insisted. "And you'll live forever."

From your lips to God's ear," Old Tom replied, "I'm sure he's listening. They say he likes miracles."

To the great joy of Father Corridan, at their graduation ceremony, the dock workers chorus, with exuberant energy and revived morale sang –

"Without a song, the day would never end
Without a song, a man ain't got a friend
Without a song, the road would never bend
Without a song.
I'll never know what makes a tree grow tall
I'll never know what makes the raindrops fall
Without a song.
I'm no good at all
Without a song."

"Whom the God's would destroy – they first make mad" – describes George Williams when granted Presidential Amnesty. His angry – "Letters From a Federal Prison" – led the New York Times best-seller list that year. Thousands of enthusiastic supporters chanting – "Peace Now – No More War" – welcomed him as he walked through the Prison gate on new prosthetic legs. Speaking at "Peace Rallies" he advocated – "One World or None" with the passion and eloquence of a dedicated "True Believer". Television interviews confirmed the persuasive power and celebrity of a blind veteran leading "Peace Marchers" down Pennsylvania avenue guided by a dog. His "Million Man March for Peace" – chanting "Hell No! – We Won't Go!" – brought decorated veterans to a crowded "Peace Village" on the Washington Mall where at night, gathered around camp fires, they sang – *"Where have all the soldiers Gone"*.

Secluded in the White House, surrounded by a protective cordon of parked Buses, our "Law and Order" President – insisting there can be no order without respect for Law – ignoring citizens' right to demonstrate – to petition his government – to enjoy freedom of speech – declared a national emergency and called out the Army.

Wearing body armor, gas masks, and face shields, carrying automatic military weapons, exploding "Stun bombs" and firing tear-gas grenades, the soldiers formed a closed perimeter around the Protestors village allowing no one to exit the encampment. Blinded, choking, coughing, eyes tearing – the trapped students and veterans could not escape the white gas clouds saturating their hair and clothing. Defending their village, Protesters threw gas grenades and rocks back at the invading armored vehicles crushing their tents, overturning latrines and injuring many.

Who fired the first shot has never been determined. What is known is for sixty seconds one hundred armor-piercing bullets were fired at non-violent citizens guilty only of refusing to obey an order to disperse.

The Coroner's autopsy described twenty deaths by gunshot wounds to the backs, heads and legs of American citizens killed by a government determined to restore order by calling their lawful protest – subversive. With the back of his head blown away by a high velocity bullet, George Williams was a casualty.

His loyal and devoted guide dog "Juno" survived.

The "Posse Comitas" Act of 1878 prohibited the Military from acting as law enforcement Agents. Our President, using Federal troops to restore Law and Order – ignored that law and he, and not the demonstrators – were law-breakers. Thus breaking laws to maintain order violated the "Rule of Law – "that wise restrain that makes men free."

A government of Law and not of men – is vital to democracy – for when lawlessness becomes pervasive – dividing a nation – eroding bonds of truth and justice uniting a civil society – we have Tyranny. By waging a war on dissent our President violated Lincoln's precept – "we are a government – of the people, by the people, and for the people."

"And the light went out of my life forever" – Theodore Roosevelt wrote upon the death of his beloved wife Alice. Distraught, grieving, he fled to the Dakotas to bury his sorrow in the hard life of a Western Rancher. Unlike the President – Helen Christian found no refuge from grief. Only an exhausting Nursing routine where all patients resembled George Williams and made clear – there will be more wars – and more young boys to care for. To again experience the tragedy of a personal loss, to endure a cruelty unrelieved by hard work and deadening feelings – was more than Helen could bear.

"Beware of pity," Nurse Ann advised: "Do not confuse what you feel with love."

Helen thought for a moment, then nodded – "Yes – belief in a perfect love attracted me to someone unable to return the generosity of my heart."

Holding Helen's hand Nurse Ann continued – "the best cure for love is getting to know each other better. Only time enables us to speak truthfully. Understanding takes years. Though disappointment and heartbreak are inevitable – we go on falling in love anyway."

Some mornings Helen awoke believing she had lost her mind – not knowing what the day would bring after another sleepless night. Never fully awake – familiar faces were nameless. Short-tempered, unreasonably angry at frustrations, she feared making a fatal dosage error. Urgent messages on the P.A. system annoyed her. Suffering anxiety attacks, she became difficult to work with – the reliable Nurse Helen once was – was no more.

"Better living through chemistry" promised relief from persistent fear and depression. Sleeping pills and tranquillizers were conveniently available and Helen Christian, ignoring possible adverse reactions, found peace in the embrace of highs and lows that soon became habitual.

Energized – when high – floating on air – working longer hours – Helen felt possessed by an overwhelming joy. In love with life. Capable of everything – discovering the intoxicating world of drugs. Seeing more – feeling more – with an unrestrained urge to hug everybody – colors and sounds intensified. She recited "Mary had a little lamb her fleece was white as snow" over and over again in a compulsion that made her smile as she recalled childhood happiness where nothing bad ever happened.

When low – she had suicidal thoughts. A dark curtain descended – infecting the day with pain and sorrow without relief. Sleep walking her daily rounds – she became incapable of meeting her responsibilities – small challenges were beyond her strength until one day she "crashed".

Unable to rise from bed, unconscious, in a deep comma, her breathing sustained by a ventilator. Helen Christian was not expected to live. Her fight for life was over.

Rehab – a slow, excruciating withdrawal from drugs – a controlled nightmare tormented by Demons dancing on the walls – speaking unintelligible words as she fought against restraining straps holding her in bed. Electric fire penetrated her brain – her legs trembling – her body writhing in a prolonged convulsion called "recovery." She could not speak – protest the abuse – the disrespect to her soul. "Dear God save me" she called out in vain – only her beating heart answered – until a familiar voice replied – "Yes Helen – it's me – Ed Cronin."

For Ed Cronin – loving Helen — remembering former feelings taught him – "love is better – the second time around." He now felt the bonds of a care-giver – fulfilling the vow – "until death do us part."

Helen reacted to the healing power of Ed Cronin's presence – reviving – as she reached out to hold his hand – re-connecting to the boy she once loved, and when embraced – she again felt a part of someone she once hoped would be hers forever. Loving became an alternative to the mad world destroying her future by decreeing – war and death – instead of life.

She now knew her Life's meaning would come from the choices she made discovering what it is to be fully alive through loving with all her heart and soul. Recovering from the alcoholic haze that almost destroyed her – Helen recalled that moment, when embracing on park bench, overlooking a lake, Ed Cronin slid his hand under her sweater, cupping her breast as she cried out – Yes! – Yes! – Yes!

Ed Cronin believed Helen's sorrow will ease with time, – becoming sad sweet feelings remembering George. For grief must be grieved following the path to healing. Helen will soon accept her loss and a world where good and evil are immutable – where love's tenderness survives – though often overwhelmed by hatred and cruelty.

At the Xavier school, Ed Cronin continued Father Corridan's work teaching Stevedores how to seek justice on docks controlled by criminals delivering one hundred million dollars a year to the Mobs and the politicians they financed, – where ending corruption once seemed an impossible dream.

After Local 602's first honest election, with Dock Wallopers and Big Bill McCormack unable to re-elect the "The Pistol Local's" first "President for Life" – Joe Ryan was defeated and sentenced to six months in prison for embezzling Union funds.

Yes, Good men will continue to seek – to strive – to dare – to conquer adversity. To better the cruel circumstances of their lives – they fight and die for life, liberty and the pursuit of happiness. However there is another power greater than human sweat and strain – and dedication – and that is the inexorable force of technological change during our "20th Century of Progress". As the Spinning Loom replaced the hand-weaver – so will hand-carrying freight up from the dark holds of ships and loaded into cargo nets be inevitably displaced.

Old Tom's joy watching Stevedores vote for an honest Union was troubled. He anticipated massive job losses in a future when one Container Ship would transport more cargo than sixteen conventional Freighters reducing both costs and travel time between ports, increasing Ship owners profits.

"Look across the harbor," Old Tom advised Ed Cronin who stopped at his food cart for lunch. "Look across the Bay at Port Newark and watch the Container ships arriving every day. They will do more to end waterfront crime than a hundred honest elections. One Crane Operator, lifting forty foot Containers on and off ships, and loading them on trucks, – will replace three hundred men – and that's the God's Honest Truth if you ask me. And without a hungry desperate mob of dock workers fighting for a day's pay – shape-ups and kickbacks will be gone forever."

A prolonged mournful blast of a Tug Boat's air horn confirmed Old Tom's dire prediction. Sea Gulls, reacting to the sound, spread their wings, rising from the dock, circling overhead, their cries a perpetual lamentation for seaman lost at sea. Ed Cronin finished his lunch disturbed by Old Tom's insight.

Strolling the waterfront, watching freight unloaded by hand, greeting men he had come to love, he thought about the dock workers tragic future and his inability to change their fate.

He also thought about how the savage pity of war morally injured returning warriors – their souls stained witnessing unforgivable horrors. As true Patriots – soldiers courageously did what they were ordered to do – returning with overwhelming force their enemies' evil – sacrificing their nation's innocence at Dresden, Hiroshima, and Nagasaki. As "walking wounded" – they sought forgetfulness – banishing sorrow – struggling to overcome the pain of unspeakable grief striving to achieve closure that never happens. They maintained the guilty silence of survivors – revealing their love for the dead by touching names inscribed on stone, evoking tears and sobs and painful thoughts challenging their right to live when so many friends died fighting and dying for Freedom and Justice as an act of love and honor – not revenge or hatred. Their idealism and loyalty exploited by often incompetent leaders, they challenged their government's lies and deceptions as a moral duty – an act of conscience. And yes – one courageous Man – one true Patriot – can make a difference.

If Abraham Lincoln's "The last best hope for Man on earth" is ever to be realized – then "My Country Right or Wrong" must give way to – "My Country when it is right – and when it is wrong – set it right."

Like prayer – A poem can be a comforting hand outstretched in darkness amidst horrors we inflict on ourselves and enemies – giving voice to the past saying – *Lest we forget – lest we forget*

"In Flander's Fields
the Poppies grow
between the crosses
row on row.
That marks our place
and in the sky
the larks, still bravely singing fly
scarce heard amidst the guns below.
We are the dead. Short days ago
we lived, felt dawn, saw sunset glow
loved and were loved and now we lie
in Flander's Fields.
Take up our quarrel with the Foe
to you with falling hands we throw
the Torch, be yours to hold it high.
if Ye break faith with us who die
we will not sleep though Poppies grow
in Flander's Fields."

About the Author

After a sixty year career as a writer-director of many award-winning films and television programs, Norman Weissman has written five novels and a memoir. Determined to oppose the silence in which lies become history, the author makes his reply in art to tell of all he has witnessed.

He lives in Brookline, Massachusetts with his wife Eveline.

CPSIA information can be obtained
at www.ICGtesting.com
Printed in the USA
BVOW08s2200290318
512016BV00002B/19/P

9 780996 616911